SHADES OF BLU

A.M. MORNING

Shades of Blu
Copyright © 2022 by A.M. Morning.

Qui 2 Life Publishing
34 Shining Willow Way
La Plata, MD 20646
www.qui2life.com
1 (301) 710-5219

Hard cover ISBN: 978-1-7326177-8-0

Paperback ISBN: 979-8-218-04252-3

eBook ISBN: 978-1-7326177-6-6

Library of Congress Cataloging-in-Publication

Name: A.M. Morning

Title: Shades of Blu

Edited by: A.A. Brandon, Tonitta Hopkins, and T. Lynn Tate

Cover Design by Shazzadur Rahman and Olayemi Bolaji

Qui 2 Life Publishing is not responsible for any content or determination of work. All information is solely considered as the point of view of the author.

Dedication

*To my beloved grandparents, thank you
for loving me always.*

CHAPTER 1

WHO AM I?

My earliest memory is of me, as a three-year-old, holding on to the black railing that ran up the bright yellow wall as I climbed the stairs to my grandparent's room. My granddaddy, Walter Lewis, was my superhero. Growing up, he would be the only man I thought could do no wrong, and he loved me more than life itself. My granddaddy was a truck driver and drove tractor-trailers from state to state.

My grandma, Vera Helen Lewis, used to be a domestic servant. After I was born, she became a stay-at-home grandma. She was so giving and caring with me, but make no mistake; she was sweet but stern.

Then there was my mom, Patricia. She was the oldest of my grandparent's four kids. My mom was a control freak and the real bitchy type. She wanted everybody to do what, when, and how she said it. Being the oldest, my grandparents would always leave her in charge, which is probably why she thought she was an adult when she had me at fourteen.

My mom had two younger brothers, Jimmy and Bruce.

Jimmy was the elder of the two and was named after my granddaddy, James Walter Lewis II. Uncle Jimmie was a casanova, and he stayed in trouble. He got whippings almost every day but was quick to run from fights. He described himself as "a lover, not a fighter."

Uncle Bruce, on the other hand, was a basic hard-hitting boy. Playing sports was his favorite pastime. His favorites were football, wrestling, baseball, and basketball. Bruce was nice with his hands too, and he loved to fight. Nobody bothered him either. Honestly, if you saw him, you wouldn't have bothered him either. Bruce was smart too and thought no one was smarter than him. He was often called a smartass, but I thought that was a good thing.

The baby of the family was my mom's only sister, Florence, and she milked it for everything it was worth. Now, Aunt Flo was a brat and a real pain in the ass. She had a notorious mean streak and was an instigator. She would get my mom and uncles in trouble just to see them get a whooping for GP (general principle).

My mom was different. She lived her life out of a Harlequin romance novel. She was boy crazy, at least that's what my grandmother called it. It's funny because my grandmother used to say that my mom was boy crazy, but my aunt was just a fast ass. What's the difference, you ask? Well, you could be boy crazy but not have the skills to secure what you want. When you're a fast ass, you know how to move to get what you want without getting caught up. The difference between my mom and my aunt was my mom chased the boys, but the boys chased my aunt. My mom didn't have the skills my aunt had, and she got caught up.

My mom used to babysit for this lady, Julie, who had a five-year-old son and lived a few houses down from my grandparents. One summer, Julie's brother, Derrick Moore, came to stay with her for a while. Everybody called him Dee. He was six feet tall with pecan tan skin, coal black wavy hair, and hazel eyes. He didn't have much in the muscle department, but he had a gorgeous smile and dimples.

Dee was one of the older kids in the neighborhood and was well liked by the younger ones. He was a laid back chill type of guy with the gift of gab. He thought he was cool, but really, he was the country bama that talked too much. Anytime you come outside to play kickball in dress shoes, yeah, that's what we called a bama move right there. It's almost like he didn't know what to wear to go outside and play. He knew good and damn well in the country they went barefoot.

When my mom first saw Dee, she thought he was cute and immediately started crushing on him. He wasn't inter-ested in her, though. He set his sights on another girl in the neighborhood named Alice. She was well liked because she loved to have fun and laughed all the time. Alice had a coke-bottle figure and was two years older than my mom. Dee was smitten by Alice, but my mom was determined to break that up.

One day, my mom decided to make a move like she had read in one of her romance novels. She was going to seduce Dee and make him hers. So, she skipped school on a rainy day and went up the street to get what she wanted from him. Dee just wanted to use his hands and 'finger bang,' but my mom wasn't having it.

She said, "I'm not wit' that finger popping jive."

So, Dee looked her in her eyes and obliged her. Suppos-edly it happened just once with Dee, but as we all know, it only takes one time.

In case you haven't figured it out, Dee is my father. It's said that Dee was my mom's first, but how are you a virgin going for the "D" your first time out? That sounds like you're an old pro to me. I guess reading those books made her feel mature and capable of adult things. Unfortunately, those books got her into some real-life shit-uations that turning a page or two wouldn't get her out of.

A few months passed, and my grandmother noticed that my mom had stopped asking for sanitary napkins. My mother started her cycle when she was ten. My grandmother handed her some sanitary napkins and told her to stay away from boys. Realizing she had never had the talk with my mom, my grandmother feared that she was pregnant. So, she went to my mom to get some answers.

"Patricia, why aren't you bleeding?" she asked.

My mother didn't know what to say. Truth be told, she didn't know why she hadn't had a period either.

The next week, my grandmother made an appointment for my mom to go to the doctor. The other siblings wanted to know what was going on with my mom and why she had to go to the doctor. Back then, you wouldn't go to the doctor unless you were injured or really sick. The doctor confirmed my mom was indeed pregnant.

When they got home, my grandparents had a conversation about how my mom ended up pregnant, as my nosey ass Aunt Flo eavesdropped.

My grandmother asked, "What are we going to do?"

My granddaddy responded, "What do you mean what are we going to do? Ain't nothing to do. She's going to have the baby. I don't believe in getting rid of babies. We didn't get rid of none of ours."

So, that was that my mom was going to have a baby. My grandmother called a family meeting and announced it to the rest of the family, but my aunt and uncles didn't seem to be bothered by it much.

My mom told Dee that she was pregnant.

He asked, "Well do you want to get married?"

She said, "No. I don't love you. My daddy said that I don't have to marry you if I don't want to."

Dee was relieved and happy. He only asked because he thought it was the right thing to do at the time. That was the last time she saw him until after I was born because a month before his 18th birthday, he enlisted in the army.

Five months later, my mother was walking home from school, and she started cramping. She got home and busted through the door hollering Aunt Flo's name. Aunt Flo came running down the stairs.

My mom said, "Flo, you gotta call momma. I'm not feeling too good."

Aunt Flo agreed, but my mom passed out in the doorway as my grandmother answered the call.

Aunt Flo blurted out, "Ma, Patricia just passed out in the doorway. She said she's not feeling well."

As calmly as she could, my grandmother said, "Ok, calm down. Your dad is on his way home and should be walking through the door shortly."

Before Aunt Flo could hang up the phone, my grand-daddy appeared. He was shocked to find my mom lying across the threshold with a small puddle of blood pooling under her. He called for my uncles, who were upstairs and unaware of what was going on downstairs. My granddaddy and uncles moved my mom to the car as Aunt Flo watched screaming and crying.

My granddaddy said to Aunt Flo, "Call your mother back and tell her that I'm on the way to the hospital with Patricia, and she should meet me there."

Somehow my grandmother ended up beating them to the hospital. My mom was still unconscious when she arrived at the emergency room. They evaluated her quickly and told my grandparents that her blood pressure was very high, putting both of us in danger. She was diagnosed with having something called preeclampsia, and an emergency C-section had to be performed to save both of our lives.

When they pulled me out, I was blue and not moving. I didn't have any signs of life at all. Immediately they started working on me. Although they finally got my heart beating again, I still wasn't crying. They gave me oxygen and put me on a ventilator. My grandparents were told I might be a special needs child due to the lack of oxygen to my brain, but I was fine. You see, they thought I wasn't crying because of possible brain damage, but what they didn't know was that the whole time God was whispering in my ear.

He said, "Don't cry, little one, I got you."

A few hours later, my mother woke up and was told she had a little girl. My mom started to smile but then felt a sharp pain in her stomach.

Grabbing her stomach, she said, "Ouch, what's going on in my belly?"

My grandmother said, "They had to cut you, baby. The doctor said that it's gonna leave a scar. No more halters and hip-huggers for you, but you'll be alright."

My mother yelled, "Got damn it! Who told him to cut me?"

It seems my mother was more worried about her appearance than my survival. She went home after a week, but I remained in the hospital for two more weeks.

Blu is the name they gave me. Once I came home, I quickly became the apple of my grandparent's eyes. As I grew up, I became the brat and instigator and inherited that notorious mean streak from Aunt Flo. We all grew up together. In fact, I thought they were my brothers and sister. That is until Aunt Flo felt enough was enough.

One day, Aunt Flo was sitting in my granddaddy's lap, and I insisted, no I demanded, that she get out of his lap.

I said, "You're in MY seat!"

Aunt Flo retorted, "He's MY father!"

I screamed, "HE'S MY FATHER TOO!"

Aunt Flo yelled back, "Tell her daddy! Tell her that you're my daddy, and you're her granddaddy."

"Got damn mufuckin bish," I screamed as I pushed her off his lap.

"Blu, you stop that," my granddaddy scolded, then continued lovingly, "Now come here. You know you're Granddaddy's baby."

That's when I found out the truth about everyone, and just like that, I went from being the youngest of five to being an only child. I then realized the power that I had over my grandparents. I was the one who made them grand, and I thought I was the Queen of the Roost.

CHAPTER 2

WALTER'S MESS

Growing up with my grandparents was sweet. I used to get everything and anything I wanted. They may not have been the richest people in the world, but they were rich in love, and they loved me. Everybody treated me extra special, even my aunt and uncles. I was so spoiled. They referred to me as "Walter's mess," the monster he created.

I always knew when my granddaddy was coming home from a trip. I would position myself in the chair at the window, waiting for him. I knew he'd come bearing gifts for me. At least that's what I expected. It didn't matter to me what the gift was. All I knew was it was something for me and me only. It was mine, and nobody was getting any. I would run and stand in the corner crying if he came into that house and didn't have anything in his hands for me. He wouldn't even be able to sit down in peace and enjoy his dinner until he went back out and got something for his little monster.

My grandmother definitely had a hand in spoiling me

too, but she'd never admit it. She once told me I was her child because she felt responsible for me being here. She didn't' think she had equipped my mother with enough knowledge about the birds and the bees, which led to her becoming a teen mom.

My granddaddy was my hero, though. I thought there was nothing he couldn't do or fix when I was a little girl. I was sadly mistaken. As I grew up, it became clear that he couldn't fix everything, but that didn't stop him from trying.

I remember when I was outside playing with these sticks in my backyard and pretending I was a ninja. This man was walking through the alley with his German shepherd he had trained to be an attack dog. The dog saw me playing with the sticks and perceived me as a threat. He ran and jumped the fence, headed straight towards me. I turned and hauled ass to the back door. I was so scared. I didn't even think to open the glass screen door and shot through it like a fireball, badly cutting my arm. It seemed like my arm was bleeding from my shoulder to my wrist. I stood there screaming at the sight of all that blood.

My grandmother screamed, "Walter! Hurry up and come here!"

My granddaddy was already on his way because the crashing sound woke him up from his nap. My grandmother ran and got clean towels to wrap my arm to try and stop the bleeding, but the blood kept soaking through, and she just kept wrapping and wrapping.

Grandma had called the ambulance but felt they were taking too long. So, my granddaddy picked me up and drove me to the local hospital, which was about ten mins away. With me in his arms, he busted through the ER doors screaming for help. The hospital staff grabbed me and rushed me to the back.

I screamed, "Help me, Granddaddy! Help me!"

My granddaddy hung his head and said, "Granddaddy can't help you this time, sweetheart."

That broke my heart because he was supposed to be my superhero.

My real parents didn't give a hoot about me. My mother dismissed my father, and he went on with his life like I didn't exist. I'm so thankful my grandparents loved me unconditionally.

New neighbors, the Crawford family, moved in across the street. They had seven children—three boys and four girls. While they were moving in, my mother set her eyes on another unsuspecting soul, the Crawford's oldest boy Michael. You would think that being a mother would have cooled her ass down, but it didn't. Instead, it started her up.

My granddaddy knew something was up when my mom started acting like a woman again instead of the child she was. She wanted to appear older to attract the attention of the Crawford boy, so she started wearing makeup. She tried to lure him by acting all sexy and sending sexy innuendos. Little did she know, he was already dating Alice. Yes, the same Alice that my father liked when my mom swooped in like a buzzard on a dead carcass. My mom and Alice were supposed to be friends, but my mother didn't care.

My granddaddy warned my grandmother about my mother's behavior.

He said, "Helen, you need to keep a tighter watch on Patricia. I see her eyeing that Crawford boy and call herself wearing makeup. Now, I love Blu, but we don't need any yellows and greens running around here."

My grandma said, "Walter, you don't know what the hell you're talking about. That girl always acts like that. She's always had an uppity way about her. Ain't nothing changed."

He said, "Helen, I don't give a damn. I don't want that nigga sniffing around here. You hear me?"

That was the end of that conversation.

The next day my grandmother noticed my mom getting up mighty early. Grandma thought she was getting up to feed and dress me because that was her regular routine. But she didn't have time to do that this particular morning. My mom had gotten up early to get out the house before the Crawford boy did so they could walk to school together.

My grandmother noticed my mom hurry out the door. Maybe she noticed because I was screaming at the top of my lungs when my mother left.

"Mama," I yelled.

My granddaddy had left for work about an hour prior, but if he had heard me screaming like that, he would have jacked her up. He always told my mom her main responsibility was taking care of me and going to school in that order.

My grandmother came downstairs to find me standing in the bay window screaming. I know my mom heard me, but she didn't even bother to look back once that Crawford boy came out the house. She just walked off out of sight. When I couldn't see her anymore, I threw a tantrum and flipped back out of the windowsill. It was a good thing my grandmother was there to catch me. I would have hit my head and had brain damage for real. It was at that moment my grandmother realized that my granddaddy was right.

To herself, she said, "Damn, Walter was right. Her ass is hot like a dog in heat!"

My mom was changing, and everyone was noticing. She started coming home from school later and later. One day, my grandmother was in the kitchen cooking. She looked up at the clock to check the time, and it was 5 p.m. She knew Walter would be home soon, and she wanted to have dinner ready by the time he got home.

Then it dawned on her, where the hell was Patricia? She hadn't seen her hit that door seal yet. Grandma was steaming. She told my mom that she couldn't do any after school activities because she had to come home and take care of me. Walter walked in the door, and everybody was home except my mom.

"Where is Patricia?" he asked as he picked me up and started bouncing me on his knee.

"I don't know where that child is," my grandmother replied. She continued, "Lord, Walter, it's getting late!"

"Come on, Helen. The kids are hungry. So, let's just eat. If she isn't home after supper, then I will go look for her. She probably at the school hanging out with them cheerleader girls. You know she wants to be a cheerleader."

My grandmother quipped, "Yea? She should have thought about that before she opened up her legs."

Grandma picked me up, put me in the chair, and called the other kids down for supper. Everyone was sitting at the table, and Granddaddy was about to say grace.

Aunt Flo asked, "Where's Patricia? Is she still walking with that Crawford boy?"

She was being funny, but then my uncle Bruce chimed in.

He said, "She ain't with that Crawford boy. He's at

home. Patricia cut third period and went with Alice downtown."

My granddaddy jumped up from the table and yelled, "WHAT!"

"Oh, Lord Walter! You got to go find this child," my grandmother screamed.

My granddaddy grabbed his keys and was headed out the door when my mom came waltzing through the door in a daze with a goofy smile on her face.

"Where have you been, Patricia?" my grandmother asked.

"I was out." She replied.

"I know you was out, but where the hell have you been?" my grandmother affirmed.

"I don't have to tell you. I'm grown," she snapped.

My granddaddy said, "The hell you are!" He continued as he took off his belt. "You a child with a child living in my got damn house!"

My grandmother snatched the belt out of his hand.

She yelled, "I'm fixin' to whip the horse shit out of you."

My mom ran upstairs with my grandmother in hot pursuit. She tried to shut the door on her, but my grandmother busted the door open.

My grandmother said, "I'm gonna ask you this one more time, Patricia. Where have you been?"

"Aw, Mama, I was out," my mom said.

My grandmother drew back and hit my mother with the belt across her arm and back. WHAP!

My grandmother said, "I'm gonna ask again."

"Aw, Mama, I was with Alice."

"What were you doing with Alice?"

My mom was about sixteen, and Alice was a couple of

years older than her, so there was no telling what they were out doing.

My mother started again, "Aww, Ma."

She couldn't even get her full sentence out before my grandmother drew back and delivered another blow of the belt. WHAP!

Aunt Flo stood at the door watching all the action.

My grandmother turned to her and said, "Go get Alice and tell her to come here."

Aunt Flo went running. That's how she got her name. They called her Flo because she ran fast like water. She was the fastest thing around our neighborhood at the time. Not even a dog could catch her.

My mom started screaming, "No, Flo! Don't do it, Flo!"

"What were you doing cutting school?" my grand-mother asked as she struck her three more times with the belt.

WHAP, WHAP, WHAP! My mom got more licks for cutting school, but the more licks she got, the angrier she became. She swung at my grandmother and missed. My mom made the mistake and forgot who she was. My grand-mother went ballistic and started tearing that ass up. My mom was screaming, swinging her arms, and kicking as my grandmother beat her with the belt. I ran into the room crying.

Grabbing my grandmother's leg, I screamed, "Stop hitting my mama!"

My mom yelled, "Stop, Mama, stop! I went out with Alice to meet up with some men!"

She finally confessed. My grandmother saw red as she whipped my mom good. My mom continued to kick and scream until she accidentally kicked me. I went flying across the room. My uncles ran to make sure I wasn't hurt as I laid out on the floor screaming. At this point, my granddaddy came into the room.

"That's enough, Helen. That's enough," he said, trying to pull my grandmother off my mother.

My grandmother, unfazed, kept on beating my mom.

He grabbed the belt from my grandmother's hand and said, "Got damn it, Helen! I said that's enough!"

Mad and out of breath, my grandmother paused.

"Damn it, Walter, I'm going to kill this child," she said before turning to my mom and saying, "You're punished forever."

Granddaddy took me out of my uncle's arms.

Trying to soothe me, he said, "Come here, sweetheart, stop crying. Granddaddy's here."

I put my arms around my granddaddy's neck and clung to him for dear life. He knew I was scared.

As my granddaddy walked out the door, he turned to my crying mother and said, "You need to get something else on your mind other than boys. I done told you that the only thing you need to worry yourself with is this child and your schooling. In that order!"

He shut the door and headed downstairs with me in his arms. Then there was a knock at the front door. It was Aunt Flo.

She said, "Open the door. It's me. I got Alice with me, Mama."

My grandmother opened the door.

"Come on in, Alice, and have a seat. I'm just going to get right down to it. I don't like the fact that you are taking my daughter with you to meet up with your men friends."

Alice said, "Mrs. Lewis, what are you talking about?"

"I'm talking about this evening when you and Patricia were out running the streets," my grandmother said.

Alice replied, "No, Ms. Lewis, you have it all wrong. I took Patricia to the free clinic because she thought she might be pregnant."

"What?" my grandmother yelled.

She wasn't ready to hear that and almost fainted.

My granddaddy hung his head low and asked, "What did you say, Alice?"

"Mr. and Mrs. Lewis, Patricia is expecting again," Alice said.

My grandmother turned to Aunt Flo and said, "Go get your sister."

Aunt Flo scampered past Uncle Bruce and Uncle Jimmie on the steps to her and my mom's room, where my mom sat sulking on her bed.

When Aunt Flo opened the door, my mom screamed, "Close the door, Flo!"

Aunt Flo said, "Mama wants to see you downstairs."

"She won't be seeing me for a long time because I'm moving out," my mom said.

Aunt Flo didn't pay my mom any mind.

"OK, but for now, mama wanna see you downstairs," Aunt Flo said as she hurried back downstairs.

She wanted to get a good seat for what was about to happen next. Aunt Flo didn't even warn my mother that Alice was downstairs, and the whole family knew she was pregnant again.

When my mom got to the bottom of the steps, she looked up and saw Alice standing there mad with her arms folded.

"Patricia, how could you lie like that and hang me out to dry with you? What is this nonsense? You said your mother knew you were going to the clinic," Alice exclaimed.

My mom sat on the steps and started crying.

She said, "I'm grown. I don't need y'all no more. I will go to the welfare office, and they will help me take care of my babies."

My grandmother didn't even look up at her.

She calmly said, "You're grown? Well, pack your shit and get out! This baby barely out of diapers, and you're pregnant again? I want your ass out of my house."

My granddaddy slowly got up from the table and walked over to my mother. My aunt and uncles started backing away from her, bracing themselves against the wall. Everybody got scared as he moved about. They didn't know what he was gonna do.

My granddaddy said, "Who's the baby's father?"

She looked up with her eyes full of tears and said, "Michael Crawford."

Granddaddy turned and directed his anger toward my grandmother.

He said, "Ain't dat a bitch!"

Granddaddy wouldn't let my grandmother kick my mom out. My grandmother was so upset and disappointed. My mom wasn't even eighteen yet, but already on her second child. Wasn't the first one enough?

My grandmother took the blame for my mom having me but said, "I'll be damned if I take the blame for this second baby. You should have known better this time around."

Granddaddy was hurt too. He wanted more for his child than what she wanted for herself. He had high hopes for her. He thought maybe one day she would go to college and become a doctor, but having a bunch of babies was not the way to become a pediatrician.

Granddaddy told my mom, "We're not going to let this one slide. Michael is going to have to do something about his responsibilities."

CHAPTER 3

F-O-O-L

A week or two passed before my mom told Michael she was expecting her second child and that he was the father. She had to prepare herself for his reaction to the news. Although he had professed to love her more than the breath he breathed, she wasn't sure of his intention. He told her he wanted to be with her forever and a day, but she was still nervous about telling him.

My mom finally decided to just come out and tell him, letting the chips fall where they may. She convinced herself she didn't care. If Michael decided to reject the idea of becoming a father, then welfare could help her take care of her babies. She was grown now and didn't need anybody. At least that was her thinking.

The next day as Michael and my mom walked across the empty football field on the way to school, she stopped right under the goal post where he first kissed her.

Holding his hand and looking into his eyes, my mom said, "SCORE!!! You're going to be a daddy."

Michael stood with a blank stare as if his mind went

straight outer space. I mean, it was some far-out news she gave him.

Finally, he checked back in and said, "OK."

He decided to drop out of school, get a GED, and join the military. Then he asked my mama to marry him. She was over the moon with herself. She finally snagged one, her very own prince charming.

When she got home, she couldn't wait to share the news with my grandparents. My grandmother was happy!

"Good, he can take care of you now, and you can get the hell out of my house," my grandmother said.

But Granddaddy wasn't as supportive.

He said, "Patricia, you're making a mistake. You don't have to marry that boy if you don't want to. We will help you take care of this child just like we're helping you take care of Blu."

My grandmother snapped back, "Like hell, we will, Walter! If this child wants to ruin her life and keep bringing children in this world that she doesn't have a clue how to take care of, that's on her! She is not going to burden me with that. The only thing she seems to be good for is opening her legs. And if she thinks the welfare system is going to help her raise these chir'ens, then so be it. Let her get her ass out there and struggle with the rest of us."

"Stop it, Helen," my granddaddy demanded.

"You stop it, Walter. If you think I'm gonna be spending the rest of my life raising Patricia's babies, you a liar and a sack of shit!"

My mom couldn't take anymore.

She yelled, "Stop it! Just stop it! I love Michael, and no matter what you say, Daddy, I'm gonna marry him!"

"Well, good!" Helen yelled.

Granddaddy shook his head and said, "Well, you a stupid, dumb fool!"

He turned and walked away, and that was that.

My mom got married a month after my baby sister was born. Michael had dropped out of school, got his GED, and enlisted into the Army. For the first year, while Michael completed basic training, my mom and little sister continued to live at home with my grandparents. When Michael came into town on his breaks, he lived with us. After completing all his training, Michael and my mom got their first apartment home together, where they and my little sister lived.

Where was I, you ask? There was no room for me in her fantasy. She left me for her dream life with him, just as she had done that day I stood screaming for her in the windowsill. It didn't matter to me because I didn't want to go with her anyway. When I did visit, I wouldn't stay a full night with them. It was ok for me to visit her during the day, but when night came, it was time for me to go home. My place wasn't with her. It was with my grandparents, who in my mind were my real parents.

Life, in the beginning, was so sweet until my mother met Michael Crawford. That's when she forgot all about me. I never felt like I was part of their family. I was a Lewis, and they were the Crawfords.

After my mama got married, she embraced the Crawford name. She said she wanted all her children to have the same last name. She hated being a Lewis. She always wanted to be something else. Anything was better than a Lewis to her. I didn't have the Crawford name. I guess that's why she treated me like I wasn't her child. I didn't care. I didn't want to be a stinky old Crawford anyway. I was proud to be a Lewis and proud of my granddaddy.

Within the next two years, my mom had another child waiting in the winds to be born. Michael told my mom that he was being deployed and sent my mom back home to stay with her family while he was overseas. So, here comes my mom back home with her belly sticking out.

Then one day, the military police showed up at our door looking for Michael. My grandmother answered the door, and the officer showed her a warrant giving them permission to come in and search the premises.

"What's this about officers?" Grandma asked.

One of the officers replied, "Ma'am, Private Crawford is AWOL."

My mom came out the back holding their youngest child and said, "Oh no, officer, he's not AWOL. He's deployed overseas. There must be some mistake. He sends me letters every couple of weeks from Germany."

The officers looked at each other and then back at my mother.

"Ma'am, do you have any of those letters with the envelopes they were sent in?"

"Of course," my mother said.

The officer asked, "Can you get them for us, please?"

My mom went into the other room, retrieved one of the letters, and gave it to the officers. They looked it over.

Then the officer said, "Ma'am, we have to take this in for evidence."

"Why?" my mom asked.

The officer went over to my mother and said, "Look at the postmark. This letter was sent from your local post office. I'm sorry to tell you this, ma'am, but Private Crawford is not overseas and seems to be right here in the neighborhood from the looks of things."

As the officers left, my mother broke down in tears crying.

My granddaddy and Aunt Flo came in from the grocery store not too long after the officers left. Grandma told Granddaddy what had happened.

My granddaddy banged his fist on the table and shouted, "Got dammit! You better pray that the police catch him before I do. I'll slit his damn throat if I ever see him again!"

Aunt Flo chimed in, "I can find him for you, Daddy."

My grandparents agreed, and Aunt Flo put the word out in the neighborhood that she was looking for her brother-in-law.

About a month later, the next-door neighbor told my granddaddy she was visiting her girlfriend a few blocks over and saw Michael coming out of another neighbor's house. She said she called out his name, and he turned around. When he saw who had spotted him, he took off running like he was O.J. Simpson. She couldn't wait to tell Aunt Flo and my granddaddy.

Granddaddy wanted to go over there immediately, but my mother begged him to let her handle it.

My mom said, "Daddy, you ain't got nothing to do with this."

Granddaddy said, "Like hell, I don't. That's my name on that damn car."

See, Granddaddy cosigned for the car as a wedding gift for my mom and Michael.

Granddaddy continued, "If we don't do nothing else, we're gonna get that car and bring it back for you and your kids."

So, my mom, Aunt Flo, and my granddaddy went over to where Michael was said to be staying with the other woman. Aunt Flo went to commandeer the vehicle because she had a driver's license, and my mom didn't.

Aunt Flo and my mom went up to the door and knocked. The woman's mother answered the door, and my mom asked to talk to Michael.

The lady called, "Mikey, somebody's at the door for you."

When Michael came out, he was shocked to see my mom and Aunt Flo at the door.

Aunt Flo looked at him and said, "We came for the car nigga."

"Flo, this ain't got nothing to do with you." Michael retorted.

Aunt Flo said, "Nigga, I'm just here to get the car. I could care less about the shit you doing to Patricia."

Michael looked out the door and saw Granddaddy in the car. He knew my granddaddy didn't play and carried a gun.

"Patricia," he said as he gave the keys to my mom.

My mom snatched the keys and said, "It's over. I don't want to talk to you, Michael."

She walked over to Granddaddy's car and jumped in, leaving Aunt Flo standing on the front porch of that lady's house.

Michael ran behind her, "Please let me explain. Let me talk to you."

Aunt Flo turned around and shouted at my mom, "Bitch gimme the keys!"

Aunt Flo ran and took the keys from my mother, leaving Michael standing at the car window trying to get my mom to talk to him.

Granddaddy calmly said, "Get away from the car Michael."

"Come on, Patricia. Please let me explain," Michael begged.

"I said get away from the car," Granddaddy firmly repeated himself as he reached over my mom's lap to roll up the window.

Michael stood watching as my granddaddy drove off. Aunt Flo was right behind them, driving my mom's car.

As Aunt Flo passed Michael, she screamed out the window, "Got damn mufuckin bish."

Turns out Michael lied to my mother and started staying with another woman because he got tired of paying bills and being responsible.

CHAPTER 4

BOX OF ROCKS

By the time my mother was twenty, she was separated and standing alone with three girls. My mom now knew she would be living with her parents longer than she anticipated.

The recent events caused her to change her attitude towards the Lewises. When she was with Michael, she walked around with her head in the clouds and an uppity attitude. Michael was her military Prince Charming, the one that was going to take her away from her dreadful family. That is until he was exposed as the lying, cheating, woman chasing, dirt dog he was. This was a reality check, and my mom realized that she needed to pull herself up by her bootstraps and get a job.

My mom learned how to drive, got a job, and went to night school to get her GED. My granddaddy was proud of her for the way she stepped up to the plate and focused on what she needed to do. I started looking up to my mom, and I loved having her around. I thought we had the best mom in the world.

What everyone missed was that she was still that lonely

little girl trying to find her way in life, except this time, she had kids tagging along. She never had much of a social life because she was all into herself or some man. She always thought she was better than everyone else and acted all high sadity.

My mom wasn't savvy at all when it came to men, especially when it came to dating them. She would let a nigga run game on her simply out of desperation. Hell, she kept letting Michael come in and out of her life whenever he wanted to.

My granddaddy used to tell her, "Child use your head for something else other than a hat rack."

I didn't know what he meant by that—it didn't make sense to me at the time. Then again, half the stuff my mom did didn't make sense to me either--for example, the time she bought a box of rocks instead of getting our school clothes out of layaway.

It was two weeks before school was starting, and she was dating this guy named George she'd met through one of her older cousins. This nigga was bad news, and you could tell he was a slickster by the way he talked. He was always trying to double talk somebody. Somehow, he was able to talk my mother into writing him checks and giving him money.

One time, he claimed he needed money to pay his union dues for a job it seemed like he never went to. Whenever he was asked what kind of work he did, he would say, "a little bit of this and a little bit of that."

"What are you paying union dues for?" my granddaddy asked him.

We could never get a real answer out of him, and my granddaddy didn't like him at all. He thought he was too old for my mother and hated that he never gave you a straight answer about anything. Granddaddy despised liars, and so did I.

One day, my mother and George went out to pick up our school clothes, which were on layaway. When they came back, he was carrying this big ass box that read Xenith 27-inch Colored TV.

My granddaddy said, "Look at this shit here. Ain't nothing in that damn box. He's carrying it too lightly."

My mother busted in the door, all proud, and said, "Sit it over there, George!"

We were all standing around the table, wondering what was in this big box.

"What is this, Ma?" me and my sisters asked.

She said, "Well, I decided to take the layaway money and surprise you guys with a TV instead."

"What about our school clothes?" I asked.

"Well, I'll go back and get them in two weeks. I got you all something better than new school clothes," she said.

Not in my opinion. I was going into the 2nd grade at the time. In her mind, she had done something great. I didn't care nothing 'bout no damn TV. I didn't want to go back to school in the same clothes I played in all summer long. They were raggedy and all torn up. The first days of school were the important days. Kids got to show off their new threads. Not to mention, that seemed like the only time of the year I would get new clothes. My mom wasn't worried about how I felt. All she cared about was showing off the new TV, all thanks to George.

As the story goes, George saw a friend of his who was selling stolen merchandise. He told my mom the dude was legit and that he had some TVs for sale. Now, he was supposed to be taking this woman to get her children's school clothes out of layaway, but he decided to take a detour over to his buddy's house, who just so happened to be selling hot TVs. What does that smell like to you? Some shit if you ask me.

George sat the box on the table with all of us standing around, peering, waiting for her to unveil this 27-inch Xenith colored TV set with remote control, which was unheard of back then. By this time, the suspense was killing us. My mom ripped open the top of the box, pulled the flap open, and looked in the box. She gasped like she had the wind knocked out of her.

George grabbed the box, and looked in it, then said, "Ain't that a bitch! Baby, I can't believe he did this!"

Everybody started looking in the box, but I was too little and couldn't see.

I kept saying, "Let me see the TV, Ma."

Granddaddy said, "Ain't no damn TV in there, Blu! Your mama spent the layaway money on a box of rocks."

George kept saying, "I can't believe he did that."

My granddaddy said, "Oh yes, you can." He turned to my mom and continued, "If you believe this nigga's shit, then you are a stupid, dumb fool! Can't you use your head for nothing besides a hat rack?"

Crying, I said, "You mean ain't' no TV, no remote control, not even an antenna in there? And we ain't got no school clothes? I ain't never going to school again."

I thought it was the end of the world. I didn't have any new school clothes. I was content to be a second-grade dropout. As I cried, my sisters started to cry. I didn't know why they were crying. My youngest sister didn't even go to school. I guess they were crying because I was crying.

My granddaddy said, "Stop crying. You'll get your new school clothes."

He got the receipt from my mother and took my aunt with him to get our school clothes out of layaway.

When my granddaddy returned with our school clothes in hand, I was jumping up and down.

Still crying, I said, "That's my granddaddy!"

He always saved the day, nothing short of a superhero. While he was out getting the clothes out of layaway, George and my uncle Bruce went looking for the guy who sold my mom those rocks.

When they came back, my uncle said, "Man, we couldn't find the dude."

My granddaddy said, "You ain't never gonna find him either." Then he turned to my mother and said, "Him and George already divvied up your money. You will never see that money again, but I want my money back," referring to the money that he paid to get our clothes out of layaway.

Over the next few weeks, my mom kept asking George did he catch up with his friend? Instead of George catching up with his friend, he dropped my mom like that hot box of rocks that he sold her. That was the last we ever heard of George.

Aunt Flo was cracking up.

She said, "How can your mom be that naive? She thinks she's all that but is always getting played!"

My mom did think she was all that because she was working and bringing home a little bit of money. Now, Aunt Flo was nothing like my mother. She didn't give niggas money; she took their money. She called it 'skinning them.' I think she got that from my grandmother. I called it, 'how to play a nigga.'

CHAPTER 5

CAN'T WE ALL JUST GET ALONG?

My aunt Flo was a wild child. She had fire in her eyes and wheels on her heels. She skated through life as if nothing ever bothered her and was afraid of nothing. I really admired her and enjoyed how mean she was to other people. She was a real scrapper, and she didn't care. You were going to get dealt with if you disrespected her.

I often wondered why Aunt Flo and my mom could never get along. They should've been each other's best friend. Instead, there always seemed to be bickering between them. I remember when I was around seven years old, my mother got her first apartment on her own through the section-8 program. We were so happy because we lived ten minutes away from our grandparents, and my sisters and I had our own room to ourselves.

Our room was huge. It was like a big playground just for us. We only had a set of bunk beds in there, so there was plenty of open space. I slept by myself on the bottom bunk, and my sisters shared the top bunk. Most of the time, my baby sister slept with my mom, except for when she had company. You know how that goes.

My aunt, uncles, and my mother's cousins would come over, and we would have what you call a set, which meant a little get-together or a little party. During one particular set, a friend of the family, Ernie, came over with Aunt Flo and Uncle Jimmie. I'm not sure what happened, maybe they had too much to drink, but Ernie stayed behind when my aunt and uncle left. I think it was all a setup, if you ask me.

So, my sisters and I were playing and running around in our room when Ernie came in and told us to go to bed like he was somebody's damn father. That was the moment I knew I hated that nigga. It sparked some dislike for my mother within me because she didn't say a word like we were supposed to listen to him. To me, he was another nigga looking for a hand-out and a hang out. He knew he was getting some that night, and the way my mother was acting, I knew it too. She was literally letting this man take control of her household like he lived there.

He left the next morning before my granddaddy picked us up. My granddaddy would pick us up every morning. He'd drop my mom at the Metro station so she could go to work, and we'd stay at my grandparent's house until it was time to go to school.

As soon as he dropped my mother off at the metro station, I said, "Ernie was over our house last night."

My granddaddy said, "For what?"

I said, "I don't know. Everybody else left, and Ernie stayed."

My granddaddy just shook his head and said, "Mhmm, that nigga."

I knew Granddaddy was going to have a serious talk with my mother because she was still married to Michael.

Ernie lived a few houses up from my grandparents and often came over to hang with my aunt and uncles. When me and my sister got to my grandparent's house after school, Ernie was there hanging out. I was so disgusted when I saw him. The irritation of him from last night flooded me all over again. I rolled my eyes at him. I mean, who did he think he was, trying to act like somebody's father.

I threw my bookbag down and went to sit down beside my granddaddy.

My granddaddy asked, "What's wrong, Blu?"

Being the spoiled little girl I was, I said, "I don't like Ernie. He was trying to act like he was our father. He yelled at us and made us go to bed."

My granddaddy looked at me through his coke bottle glasses that made his eyes as big as a bug's eye and raised his caterpillar eyebrows.

He turned to Ernie and said, "That's their damn house. You don't tell them what to do and when to go to bed. You don't live there, and you are not these kid's father."

My granddaddy was furious because he knew that Ernie was coming to the house messing around with Aunt Flo, and now he's messing with my mama. My granddaddy was not having that. He was a very stern and honest man and a straight shooter known for cussing people out. Most people feared him because he didn't take shit from nobody except my grandmother. She was the only one who could call him an old mother fucker and get away with it.

Aunt Flo looked at Ernie and said, "Oh, so you spent the night at her mama's house?"

She got up and walked outside, and Ernie followed her like a little puppy.

I thought to myself, "Well, my job is accomplished. He won't be telling me to go to bed no more."

When my mother arrived at my grandparent's house, we were all in the living room watching TV. My aunt was leaning on the arm of the love seat, and Ernie was sitting beside her. My mom went over and squeezed next to Ernie on the other side. I don't know what Ernie and my aunt talked about, but when my mother started rubbing on his knee to say hi, he rejected her.

He said, "Get off of me!"

Confused, my mother said, "What? Why?"

He said, "Because I don't want nobody touching me."

My mother said, "Well, Flo's touching you."

Rudely he said, "So what, I like her. I don't like you."

My mother jumped up in a huff.

Upset, she said, "Nigga, don't bring your ass over my house no mother fucking more!"

He said, "I don't care! Your shit wasn't good no way!"

My granddaddy was in the back laying down, but when he heard the arguing, he got up and came to the living room. My mom was yelling and cussing at Ernie.

Granddaddy asked my mom, "What is going on, and what's wrong with you?"

She said, "Nothing, daddy, nothing!"

Aunt Flo interjected, "She just mad because Ernie told her to get off him when she was leaning on him."

Granddaddy said, "I don't know what you're getting all mad for. This boy been coming down here every day chasing your sister."

My mom said. "What? I didn't know that."

Granddaddy snapped back, "There's a lot you don't know! I keep telling you, use your head for something other than a hat rack!"

My mother went outside with tears in her eyes. My aunt followed behind her, and I followed behind my aunt. They went to the side of the house.

My mother looked at me and said, "Take your ass back in the house.

My aunt chimed in, "With your grown-ass self. She was the one that told daddy about Ernie spending the night at your house."

I knew how to listen. I turned my little ass around and went back in the house. Once in the house, I went straight to my grandmother.

I said, "Grandma! They out there 'bout to fight!"

Grandma said, "What? Where they at?"

I said, "On the side of the house by your bedroom."

My grandmother went straight to the window in her bedroom. I knew she was going to eavesdrop. She was good for that. That's how she knew everything that was going on. I took my little ass to the bedroom right behind her. Shoot, I wanted to know what they were saying too.

Aunt Flo told my mother, "Listen, Ernie, don't mean nothing to me. I don't care what happened between you two. He's just one of the guys I'm dealing with right now."

My mother's feelings were hurt because Ernie turned her down in front of everybody. My mom always thought she was better than my aunt. Ernie's rejection was embarrassing, and said something different.

Aunt Flo was wild and fun to hang around. My mom, on the other hand, acted stuck up like a prude and always played the role of the shy victim. Everybody wanted to hang out and be friends with my aunt. I think that's why my mom had such animosity towards her.

My mom always had the best and the first of everything, while Aunt Flo got all her hand me downs growing up. She never got new dresses. From what I saw, it seemed to make her feel second best, like she was always runner up. Aunt Flo could never come in first with my grandparents, but with everybody else, it was the opposite. Everyone else preferred my aunt Flo over my mother. She was in first place, and my mother was just an honorable mention with her stank attitude.

My mother couldn't understand why men chased after Aunt Flo and not her. My aunt never paid a nigga any mind. To her, it was just business. She just used men to get what she wanted at the time. My mother, on the other hand, chased the fairy tale version of men from her romance novels. She wasn't going to find that type of man where we lived. All she'd get were lies, and games ran on her because of her naiveness.

These fundamental differences were the cause of many arguments between my mother and aunt.

My granddaddy would say, "You are sisters. You don't let outsiders come between family."

Ernie chased after Aunt Flo because she paid him no mind. He didn't want anything to do with my mother because she was too eager to give him all of her at one time. My aunt knew that Ernie was a hoe. He had slept with three other family members, but Aunt Flo didn't care. At that time, she didn't have a heart for him. I don't think my mother really had a heart for him either, even though she acted as if she was hurt.

I thought that day would be the end of Ernie in our family, but no. He kept chasing Aunt Flo even after she had a baby by someone else.

I believe the situation with my aunt Flo and Ernie is what eventually made my mom betray her. If my mom thought that she was so much better than my aunt—better looking, had more money, and was better versed, then why would she betray that sisterly trust and family loyalty for a nigga? I still haven't figured that out and may never know why these two sisters could never get along.

I love my family to death. As much as I loved Aunt Flo, there was a period of time we didn't get along. She didn't speak to me for some time because she thought I was this spoiled-ass bratty child. I treated her with no respect. I called her a loser, a bum, and a hoe to her face. It was inappropriate behavior for a 7-year-old. But my mother kept feeding my sisters and me negative thoughts and information about my aunt and uncles.

My mom always called her siblings bums and losers because they hung on the porch and street corners drinking and smoking weed. She expressed that this type of behavior was frowned upon. My mom always played "Ms. Goody Two Shoes" like she did no wrong, but she smoked and partooketh of the devil's nectar too. She was no different from any other young adult coming up during that time. Let her tell it, she walked on water and did no wrong.

I should have known my mother wasn't all that good. Almost every night of the week, she entertained the same people she called losers and bums at our apartment. During that time, she was drinking and smoking just like the rest of them. How could she point fingers at them when she was guilty of doing the same things? In my book, that made her a loser too. I didn't find out the whole truth about that until some years later.

I used to walk right up to my aunt, uncles, and their friends and call them losers and bums. One day while I was following and taunting them, I called my aunt Flo a fat bitch.

Aunt Flo turned and said, "What did you say?"

Before I could get bitch out the second time, she slapped the shit out of me.

Stunned, I turned and again said, "Bitch!"

She slapped me again, this time knocking me down. I was so mad. I picked myself up, brushed the dirt off, and belted out bitch again. Aunt Flo backhanded me, dropping me to my knees. As I sat there on my knees, I looked up, barely able to speak. I mustered enough energy to let one more bitch escape from my lips.

Aunt Flo raised her hand to hammer down yet another slap, but out of nowhere, my grandmother grabbed her arm.

Grandma said, "What the hell are you doing beating on this child like that? You don't be hitting no child like that. If she does something bad, you get a switch and tear her hind parts up. You're hitting on her like she a nigga on the street."

My aunt replied, "Ma, that's because she called me a bitch like I was a nigga on the street!"

"I don't care! Don't put your hands on her again," my grandmother said.

As my grandmother helped me off the ground, she noticed my tooth went through my lip. My mouth was bleeding, and my lip was swollen. I could hardly speak. It looked like I stuck my face in a beehive.

I whispered in my grandmother's ear, "Grandma, it's a good thing you came out here when you did cause I was gonna fuck that bitch up."

Grandma yanked me to face her and said, "I ought to

whoop your ass! Haven't you learned your lesson yet? Get your ass in this house."

My face was swollen for a good week and a half. I never called my aunt any derogatory names after that. Aunt Flo and I apologized to each other, but she made it clear that she would never let me disrespect her.

She explained, "I'm an adult, and you're a child. A child needs to stay in a child's place."

Based on how my grandparents raised me, I thought me and my aunt were equals. I was different from the rest of the grandchildren. I was their "fifth child."

I was always around my grandparents and adults in general. They used to call me grown because I didn't hang out with kids my age. I was grown and mischievous—a bad combination. Every now and then, I'd do things like stick metal scissors in the socket, hang my baby sister out the window by her feet, take my middle sister to the attic to get on the roof, telling her she could fly. As you can see, I was a very mischievous child, and I got my ass whooped every time.

Don't get me wrong; I loved my sisters. I thought I was their protector. I could hurt and taunt my sisters, but I wouldn't let anyone else do harm to them. That's just how my family was. We may not have gotten along and mistreated each other, but an outsider would get their ass kicked if they tried it.

CHAPTER 6

RIGHT BACK WHERE WE STARTED

Our time in our first section-8 apartment was short-lived. My mother couldn't budget her niggas and money at the same time. It would seem she cared more about partying than she did about providing for us. The rent was income based so she could take care of her three kids and keep a roof over our heads. The fact that she screwed that up showed you where her priorities were. We ended up moving right back where we started, in the den on our bunk beds at my grandparent's house. Me and my mom slept at the bottom, and my two sisters slept at the top.

I grew up in a neighborhood where all the neighbors knew each other and hung out at each other's houses from time to time. My family became really good friends with some of the neighbors, and the Beysmores were no exception. My grandparent's house was part of a three-set row house. My grandparents had one end. Our neighbor, Miss Kathy, had the other end, and the Beysmores were right in the middle. The Beysmore's house consisted of a single mother, Miss Larissa; her five children, Stacy, Big Mike,

Heavy, Man-Man, and Faye; her brother, Poppy; and a couple of her grandchildren.

Stacy was the oldest of the five. She had a son, Ray, who was around the same age as my sister Vicky. My sister was head over heels in love with that boy. Stacy was only a few years older than my mom, and they were good friends at one point.

Stacy worked for the Federal Government and helped my mom get on. She told my mother about the government program that hired people who were receiving government assistance. When Stacy's job hosted a job fair, she went to her boss and told her about my mother needing a job. Stacy came home and schooled my mom on what to do and where to go to apply. This was back in the day before Reganomics, when black people were getting into the government, getting business loans, and coming up. Then Regan cut all those programs putting a screeching halt to everything.

My mother was lucky. She got in before those programs ended. My mom was able to go to school, take clerical classes, and get a job. She was so happy, but her demeanor changed as soon as she got the job. She started acting like she was better than everyone else.

Now Faye was Stacy's only sister. Like Stacy, she had a son, and his name was Jaquan. Faye walked around as if she had a crown on her head and a throne somewhere with her name on it. If she had it her way, she would have had everyone calling her Queen Faye. In actuality, the only throne she had was a toilet bowl. She was a lot like my aunt Flo when it came to how she treated men. They shared the belief in skinning men for money. You'd think they would have gotten along, but Aunt Flo couldn't stand her ass. Faye was the competition.

Big Mike was Stacy's oldest brother, and he was the fighter of the family. He was the most respected. Everybody knew not to fuck with him because he was crazy and his temper was out of control. Watching him go off and fight people would always excite me for some reason. Big Mike would even fight his own siblings; he didn't care who it was, honestly.

I liked Big Mike, but I'm not sure if it was because of his temper or his looks. He was tall, slender, and had long wild hair. In my opinion, he was for sure the most handsome of all the Beysmore men.

Everyone referred to the Beysmore's middle son as Heavy because he was heavy in the streets. He pushed major weight selling drugs and was the main breadwinner in the house. He really didn't live there, but he was over there so much he might as well have.

The baby of the bunch and the one my aunt Flo thought was the most handsome was Man-Man. I think she had a secret crush on him because he was a badass. The Beysmore boys were known as menaces in our neighborhood. They sold drugs, robbed people, fought, stole shit, and wreaked havoc on our community. If something went down, it might not have been all of them, but you can bet your ass one of the Beysmore boys had something to do with it.

Miss Larissa's brother, Poppy, was a military veteran and had fought in the Vietnam War. He was retired from the Army but had plenty of money. Poppy really liked my aunt Flo, but you know how she is—she liked him, but she liked his money more. Aunt Flo looked at him as a friend, as we all did, but he looked at her as much, much more.

Poppy was about twenty years older than my aunt, but it didn't matter because his money spent the same. He was a kind old man who loved drinking, but he wasn't alone because Miss Larissa was a pure lush herself. Those two drank their liquor together and ran the household next door to us.

The Lewises and Beysmores were good friends, and you would have thought my mom and Stacy were the best of friends. Well, at least that's what Stacy thought. Stacy and my mom would do things together like go to the mall, go shopping for their kids together, and just hang out whenever neither of them had anything else to do. That's one thing I never really understood about my mom. She would have a good friend, and then something would always happen, and within the blink of an eye, they were no longer friends.

It would've been cool if my mom had explained what was going on between her and Stacy to the rest of the family, but I guess that would have been too much like right. Even Aunt Flo didn't know why my mom suddenly changed her attitude towards Stacy. My mom would see Stacy coming and then turn her head the other way saying how much she couldn't stand her. I thought it may have been because Stacy drove a fancy car, but my mom had to catch the bus back and forth to work—never mind the fact they had two different schedules.

My grandparents even noticed that she had stopped hanging out with Stacy. According to the rumor mill, it was because of some guy at work that my mom was crushing on. Instead of him returning those feelings to her, he crushed on Stacy instead. So, my mom didn't want to kick it with Stacy anymore. I know it sounds crazy, but that was classic Patricia. She always liked men who were either not into her or belonged to someone else—got damn mufuckin bish.

One day, the siblings decided to get together and give my grandparents a surprise anniversary party. That party was awesome. Everybody was there. All my grandparent's friends, family, and neighbors that lived in the area came. Some people even came from Baltimore and Virginia.

At the time, we were really close with the Beysmores. We all hung out together. We would have cookouts together and alternate houses to play cards. Everything was cool until the night of the anniversary party. Stacy showed up with Faye, Big Mike, and Man-Man. Heavy had gotten popped for selling drugs and had to do some time. I never saw him again after he went to jail. Anyway, as soon as my mom saw Stacy walk in the door, she went to my aunt Flo.

My mom said, "I don't want her here. Make her leave Flo."

My mother was too chicken shit to do her own dirty work. My aunt didn't care. She didn't even question why my mother wanted this girl to leave.

Aunt Flo walked up to Stacy and said, "I'm sorry you can't stay. My sister doesn't want you here."

Stacy responded, "Why don't she want me here? What did I do?"

Aunt Flo said, "I don't know what you did, but she doesn't want you here, so you gotta go."

Stacy and her brothers all left. Since my uncle Jimmie was the one that brought them there, he left with them. We went on partying and having a good time into the early morning. That was the first time I stayed up until 5 a.m. in the morning. They found me under the table, drunk with a bottle of T.J. Swann wine. I was tearing it up.

The next day, Stacy decided that she wanted some answers. So, she met my mother at the bus stop when she got off work. Man-Man and my uncle Jimmie went with her. When my mother got off the bus, Stacy stepped in her path.

Stacy said, "Alright, Patricia, what's the problem? I thought we were friends. Why did you make me leave the party? Why couldn't I stay? What did I do to you?"

My mom became irate and started going off.

My mom said, "Don't be coming all in my face asking me all these questions like that. You already know what you did!"

Uncle Jimmie said, "Calm the fuck down!"

Before he could say anything else, my mom started swinging on him with her purse. He took one step back, punched her right in the mouth, and knocked her front teeth out. My mom screamed and ran home. She busted through the door with her mouth bleeding and her teeth in her hand. My granddaddy jumped up.

"Patricia, what's wrong with you?" he said.

Crying, my mom said, "Look what Jimmie did to me! They jumped me getting off the bus!"

My granddaddy demanded, "Who?"

My mom cried, "Jimmie, Stacy, and Man-Man!"

My grandmother, Aunt Flo, and Uncle Bruce jumped up. Uncle Bruce quickly laced up his shoes. They were about to wreck! But before they could get out the door, Uncle Jimmie ran in the house.

My mom screamed at him, showing him her missing teeth, "Look what you did to me!"

Uncle Jimmie stood beside my granddaddy.

Granddaddy said, "Jimmie did you do this?"

Uncle Jimmie said, "Wait, Daddy, let me explain!"

Granddaddy raising his voice in frustration, said, "Did you do this?"

"Yes, daddy, but let me explain," Uncle Jimmie pleaded.

Before he could tell what happened, my granddaddy stood flat-footed and cold-clocked him from the side. Uncle Jimmie spun around and hit the floor as if he were in a cartoon or something. Then he jumped up and ran out the house. By that time, the Beysmores were all standing on their porch, including Miss Larissa.

There we were, two families that were once friends, about to throw down.

Faye stood in her yard screaming, "This is all your fault, Patricia!"

My mom just stood on our porch crying and holding her bloody mouth. Aunt Flo ran off the porch into our yard and tried to reach over the low chain-linked fence to grab Faye, but Uncle Jimmie was holding her back. Eventually, Aunt Flo managed to reach around Jimmie just enough to grab a handful of Faye's hair. Now everyone was screaming at each other, and things got hectic really quick.

Uncle Bruce grabbed Uncle Jimmie so he wouldn't be in the middle of the girls. In all the commotion, nobody saw that Stacy slipped away and re-appeared with a broom. She swung the broom, and it was headed straight for Uncle Bruce's head. My granddaddy grabbed the broom in mid-swing. He yanked it so hard Stacy fell into Faye, and both girls hit the groundbreaking Aunt Flo's grip on Faye's hair. Some of poor Faye's hair was ripped out and was still in Aunt Flo's hand. Before his sisters could get up, Man-Man had jumped the fence and started swinging on Uncle Bruce.

Me and my sisters stood on the porch watching as Grandma, and Miss Larissa yelled for everyone to stop. It was chaotic. Everybody was fighting, except my mom, of course. She was still standing there crying and holding her mouth as if her tears alone would stop the fight. My granddaddy was choking Uncle Jimmie. Man-Man had my uncle Bruce in a headlock, and Aunt Flo now had Faye by the shirt trying to pull her over the fence. Miss Larissa went down to help Stacy as she tried to prevent my aunt from successfully getting Faye onto our property.

Finally, my grandmother got tired of yelling. She went into the house and returned with a twelve-gauge shotgun in her hand. I immediately grabbed my sisters and ran into the house. It was time for me to watch everything unfold from the comfort of our living room window. POW! My grandmother fired one single shot in the air. Instantly the fighting ceased. Everyone, except Faye, hit the ground with their hands spread out as if they were being arrested. Faye just stood like a deer in headlights.

My grandmother pointed the shotgun right at Man-Man, but for some reason, he didn't look scared. He didn't dare open his mouth either.

My grandmother said, "Get your ass back on your property right now, and everybody cut out all of this stupid foolishness! I want to know what the hell is going on, and I want to hear it from the top."

Grandma lowered the gun and nodded her head towards the house. That was everyone's cue to come inside. So, my mom, aunt, and uncles turned to go into the house. When Uncle Jimmie got to the door, my granddaddy put his arm out to stop him.

Granddaddy said, "Not you boy!"

My grandmother looked at my mother and said, "You either."

My mother whined, "But mama, my mouth?"

My grandmother yelled, "Flo, bring your sister a towel and some ice!"

Aunt Flo quickly came to the door and handed my mom ice wrapped up in a dishtowel. With the gun in her hand, my grandmother led the way to Miss Larissa's yard so they could hash things out. Lucky for me, they were sitting outside on the porch, and I could hear and see everything from the window.

"Alright, let's hear it, Patricia. What's the story?" my grandmother said.

Removing the towel from her mouth, my mother said, "It's nothing to talk about. She carried me at work in front of our co-workers like we weren't friends. Aunt Flo told them to leave the party last night, and then they attacked me at the bus stop."

"Stacy, is that true?" Miss Larissa asked.

"No," Stacy retorted and continued, "What happened was, we were in the cafeteria having lunch together. While we were eating lunch, a guy named Gary, that apparently Patricia had the hots for, came over and sat down. Gary asked me out on a date, and I agreed because it was a movie I wanted to see."

Stacy went on and explained how my mom got up from the table with an attitude, stomped over to the trash, and dumped her food. The kicker came when Stacy admitted that she knew my mom liked Gary, but she and Gary had been secretly dating for months and never told anyone to keep people out of their business since they worked together.

Stacy looked at my grandmother and said, "I tried to tell Patricia that we were dating before she even met him, but Patricia wouldn't listen."

My mother didn't care. In her mind, Stacy was still

public enemy number one, which meant she no longer wanted to have anything to do with any of the Beysmore family members.

My grandmother turned to my granddaddy and said, "Do you hear this? These girls are out here fighting over a damn man!"

Miss Larissa interjected, "Not a man, a boy!"

"A boy that doesn't belong to either one of you," my granddaddy said.

My grandmother said, "Listen, baby, men come a dime a dozen.

"And every ten minutes like a bus," Miss Larissa chuckled as she high fived my grandmother.

My grandmother replied, "That's right! Ain't no need in y'all having bad blood over this. Especially when it seems this was just a misunderstanding."

For the sake of their mothers, Stacy and my mother fake made up, but my mother still wanted to have nothing to do with any of them. To Stacy, my mother had become this petty little bitch that she didn't want to have anything to do with, so the feeling was mutual.

Satisfied with the appearance of them making peace with each other, my grandmother said, "Alright, the rest of you all need to make peace now. We live too close to each other to have all this mess between us."

Grandma looked over and motioned for Aunt Flo and Uncle Bruce, who had made their way back out on the porch to watch how things went down, to make their amends. My mother headed back to the house, rolling her eyes while everyone else exchanged their apologies. Although the guys genuinely apologized, Aunt Flo was just thankful she finally got a chance to lay hands on Faye. She couldn't stand that girl.

My granddaddy popped Uncle Jimmie on the arm and said, "Now you come with me. You still have some explaining to do."

Uncle Jimmie shook his head as he turned to hop the fence back to our yard.

The feud was over between most of our family, but the Beysmores were still a nuisance to the neighborhood.

One day, the homeowners in the community decided enough was enough and started a petition to have the Beysmore family removed. Of course, our family didn't sign the petition because they had never broken into our house or stole anything from us. In fact, they respected my granddaddy very much and was fearful of him. That still didn't stop the community from getting the number of signatures they needed.

The petition was filed, and shortly after, Miss Larissa came yelling and banging on our door. It felt like the crack of dawn, and she was crying and cursing at the top of her lungs. Everybody in the house tiredly got up and headed toward the living room to see what was going on. My granddaddy opened the door, and just the sight of Miss Larissa almost startled him. Tears and snot were streaming down her face, and her hair was every which way all over her head.

She said, "Walter, these motherfuckers done came to kick me out my house. I don't have nothing. Please can I move some of my stuff in your yard until the boys can come back with a truck?"

My granddaddy agreed, and we all watched as the day unfolded.

After Miss Larissa put most of her things in the yard, they weren't allowed back into the house. So, she stood in her yard and screamed all kinds of nasty things to anybody who would listen. She made such a racket that the other neighbors started to step outside into their yards or look out their windows to see what was going on.

She yelled, "Y'all bitches think y'all getting rid of us, but we'll be back! Fuck all you Mother Fuckers!

She looked like a madwoman flailing her arms with her blood-shot eyes. A car with three ladies slowed down while passing, trying to be nosey.

"What the fuck you looking at, you nosey bitches?" she yelled as she picked up a shoe from one of the boxes and hurled it at the car.

Scared, the driver sped up the street.

Miss Larissa continued her rant, "I hate each and every one of you. And everyone who signed this damn petition to put me and my family out can kiss my ass!"

She pulled her pants down and turned around to moon all the neighbors that were watching. At this point, it was clear she was hysterical. My grandmother went out to her to try and calm her down.

As my grandmother gently tugged at Miss Larissa's arm, she said, "Come on, Larissa pull up your clothes. You don't want to give them the satisfaction of seeing you come apart."

She yanked away from my grandmother and said, "No, Helen. They want a show. I'm going to give it to them."

Since my grandmother couldn't calm her down, she just walked over from time to time to comfort and rub Miss Larissa's back as she continued her rant and showed her ass literally for all the other neighbors to see. My grandmother knew if the roles were reversed, Miss Larissa would do the same for her.

Miss Larissa sat out there and acted an entire fool for what seemed like hours. She was mad at everyone who had passed judgment on her and her children, everyone who had signed that petition, and everyone who had pretended to be her friend. Her anger burned, but she knew that my family didn't have anything to do with what was going on.

Finally, someone in a moving truck pulled up. They loaded Miss Larissa's belongings into the back of the truck and drove off. The Beysmore house stayed empty for a few months; then, a new family moved in.

The Bakers were a family of five. There was Mr. & Mrs. Baker, their sons Cedric and Cecile, and their daughter Kelly. We instantly became the best of friends when they moved in. The boys were around my age, and Kelly and my sisters were around the same age. It was great having kids right next door to play with. I pretended the boys were my brothers, and to them, I was their other sister. We went to school together, played over each other's houses, and even ate dinner together from time to time.

Mrs. Baker was like a mother to me and treated me as one of her children. I actually liked the Bakers better than the Beysmores. Cedric and Cecile were so protective of me. Cedric and I were the same age, but Cecile was four years older than us. Cecile acted like he was everybody's father, but he was so timid and shy when it came to the rest of the neighborhood, especially the girls.

I didn't understand it back then, but good old Cecile was reaching puberty and becoming interested in girls. It took me and Cedric a nice little while to understand what was going on. We would tease Cecile all the time about him liking the girl across the street. Come to think of it, Cecile liked every girl on every street. He became a real coochie hound, always sniffing behind some girl, and that's how things went for a very long time.

The neighborhood had calmed down considerably now that the Beysmores were gone. We no longer heard about other neighbors being robbed or having their homes broken into. All was good, and the neighborhood was drama free. That is until the day Big Mike showed up out of his mind.

Mr. & Mrs. Baker had left the house a few hours earlier to go out and enjoy the town. They left Cecile to watch over Cedric and Kelly. Out of nowhere, Big Mike showed up high on angel dust, thinking he still lived there. He started banging and yanking on the door like a lunatic, scaring Cecile and them half to death.

Cecile and Cedric called my house for help. When I picked up the phone, I could hear Kelly crying in the background.

I answered, "Hello."

Cecile whispered, "Blu, help! My parents aren't home, and there's a crazy man at our door trying to break in."

I could hear Big Mike banging on the door in the background and yelling, "Ma! Open the door and let me in."

Cedric squealed, "Send Mr. Walter quick."

As I dropped the phone and ran to go tell my granddad, I heard Aunt Flo and Uncle Bruce outside trying to talk some sense into Big Mike.

Aunt Flo said, "Mike, your mama ain't there. She don't live there no more. Remember?"

Uncle Bruce jumped in and said, "Why don't you come over here, and we can call her."

Big Mike paid them no mind and kept banging on the door, calling for his mama. He was banging so hard I thought it was going to cave in.

A few moments later, Mr. & Mrs. Baker pulled up to see Big Mike banging and yanking on their door. Mr. Baker jumped out of the car and ran to the house.

He said, "Excuse me, Sir, can I help you?"

Big Mike replied, "No, you can't help me do nothing! I need my mother to open this damn door!" Big Mike yanked the doorknob back and forth, then continued, "Open up, Ma!"

It was all making sense to Mr. Baker now. He had heard the stories about Miss Larissa and her kids and how they had been put out a few months before he moved in.

Mr. Baker said, "Man, I'm sorry about everything that happened, but you have to leave. You don't live here no more."

Big Mike turned and said, "I ain't going nowhere!"

Mr. Baker said, "Look, man, you have to go."

Big Mike snatched Mr. Baker up by the collar and said, "I will kill you!"

The neighbor on the other side of the Baker's house, Miss Kathy, came out on her porch. She couldn't stand the Beysmores and was the one who started the petition that got them removed from the neighborhood.

Big Mike let go of Mr. Baker, shoving him back in the process. Mr. Baker quickly gathered himself and pulled out his switchblade. He thought he was ready to rumble, but that blade didn't faze Big Mike.

Miss Kathy yelled, "Get on away from here, you hoodlum, I done called the police."

Big Mike turned his head to say something to Miss Kathy,

and Mr. Baker swung the switchblade catching Big Mike in the arm opening a gash that squirted blood everywhere. Big Mike snatched the blade from Mr. Baker as if he didn't feel anything and flung the blade into our yard. He advanced toward Mr. Baker with a sinister look in his eye. You could see the fear on Mr. Baker's face as he realized Big Mike was high off something.

My family watched from the window and screen door as Aunt Flo and Uncle Bruce pleaded with Big Mike to go home.

"Big Mike, you don't live there no more, just go on home," Aunt Flo said.

"Come on, man, calm down," my uncle Bruce added.

Blood was dripping all over Big Mike's shirt and pants, but he had yet to notice it.

"Big Mike, go home," my uncle pleaded again.

"Don't tell me what to do. That's right, you can get this too," Big Mike said to my uncle, who was standing on our porch.

Miss Kathy was fed up with Big Mike's foolishness. While Big Mike continued hurling threats at Uncle Bruce and Mr. Baker, she went inside her house. She returned toting a big cast-iron skillet. Mrs. Baker saw Miss Kathy and immediately knew what she was planning to do. The problem was Miss Kathy wasn't strong enough to deliver the blow that was needed to knock Big Mike out.

Mrs. Baker made her way into Miss Kathy's yard. As Big Mike continued his rant at my uncle Bruce and Mr. Baker, he came off the porch and down into the yard. As he stood with his back next to the fence that separated Miss Kathy and the Baker's yard, Mrs. Baker drew back and swung that cast iron skillet with all her might at Big Mike's head. Big Mike, stunned, stumbled a few steps before falling flat on his face. His lights were out, and everything went quiet.

The police arrived and took statements from everyone. It was clear that Big Mike was going to jail. They handcuffed him but didn't put him in to the police car until after the paramedics took a look at that nasty gash. I heard he was arrested because he had prior charges for breaking and entering. I know I said before that I liked to see Big Mike get agitated and fight, but that night I was scared shitless.

I had never seen Big Mike so out of control. The look in his eyes was so dark and cold. I didn't know who he had become, but he wasn't the Big Mike that I once knew. We later heard that Big Mike was sent to a mental institution because the drugs he had indulged in caused him a permanent mental break. I was really sad when I heard that. Unfortunately, that would be the first of many tragedies in his entire family.

The following year Miss Larissa died. It was said that she died from a broken heart. Apparently, she was never the same after she lost her house, and then Big Mike losing his mind pushed her over the edge. Faye suffered a brain aneurysm and followed her in death. Heavy stabbed and killed someone while locked up, which gave him life in prison. Man-Man was killed by a security guard while robbing an upscale store. I heard that Poppy drank himself to death and died from cirrhosis of the liver.

The Beysmore family seemed to have dropped like flies leaving Stacy as the last man standing. When you look at her today, you can tell that life was not kind to her. She has all white hair and missing teeth and reminds you of a crackhead from the 80s. I don't know for sure, but it's possible that she started using drugs too.

The Beysmores used to have it all, and despite their issues, people used to envy them. They had a fast fairy tale beginning but a slow tragic ending. In the end, life continued for us with our new neighbors, the Bakers. It was a new beginning, and I enjoyed my new found brothers in the Baker's boys.

Chapter 7

─────────

You Shoulda Took Your Old Ass Home

My aunt Flo ran game on men like it was a sport. She had a knack for finding old perverts who wanted a young girl. She'd take all their money and leave them high and dry. I remember one Friday night, Aunt Flo and her girlfriend, Sheila, were at the liquor store, and this old man named Otis started hitting on them. He bragged about how he'd just got paid and could show them a good time.

My aunt looked at Sheila and winked. That wink meant "operation take a nigga's dollars" was a go. They felt it was their job to relieve him of his funds.

Otis asked, "What would it take for me to get an audience with you?"

Aunt Flo said, "If you get a hotel room, we'll come over. But you have to get us some get-high if that's not too much for you."

Now "get high" was code for drinks and smokes.

He bragged, "Nah, that ain't shit. I roll with big bank. I'm the foreman on my job, so I got money."

That was a dumb move on his part.

Aunt Flo said, "Ok. Well, I'm hungry, and I want to go dancing."

He was like, "Shit, I know a place. Let's go."

Otis took them to a hole in the wall joint. My aunt gave Sheila a "what the hell look."

Aunt Flo said, "Aww hell no, nigga! Come up off this shit."

Placing his hand on my aunt's back, he said, "Chill baby, we'll have fun here. This is where all the guys come and chill after they get off work. They cash their checks next door at the liquor store, then they come over here to have a few drinks before they head in. Besides, they have the best food at this greasy spoon."

All Aunt Flo heard was "cash their checks," and all she saw was the dollar signs. She knew it was time for her to go to work.

They went in, he got them a table and ordered them food. Otis bought them whatever they wanted. After a while, the place started getting crowded, and men started pouring in, ready to spend their paychecks. As Aunt Flo and Sheila mingled, they met a lot of connects. Aunt Flo felt like she was in player heaven. People were chatting them up and buying them drinks left and right. My aunt wasn't stupid, though. She and Sheila weren't drinking the drinks. They would get up to dance, set the drinks on another table, then walk away.

While Aunt Flo and Sheila were working the room, their victim patiently waited. He done ate, had some drinks, and now he was ready to go back to the motel and get the real party started.

They finally made it to the motel.

Aunt Flo said, "Wait a minute, you didn't get our weed?"

Otis said, "Yes, I did. I got it while we were at the spot. One of my partners hooked me up."

They started rolling J's and lit that room up. It's normally puff, puff, pass, but they had so much weed, they didn't have to pass. It was just puff, puff, puff.

Sheila said, "Damn, that was some good shit. Where'd you get it from?"

Otis said, "My man Danny hooked me up."

Sheila said, "Well, why don't you slide me his number? I can turn my brother on to him for his supply."

That was a lie. They wanted the number so that they could hook up with the weed man themselves. Old dude didn't care. He gave them Danny's information anyway.

Otis started pouring shots to keep the party going. After a couple of shots, Aunt Flo and Sheila started pouring the shots out when Otis wasn't looking. He was trying to get them drunk, but they were getting him drunk instead.

They kept feeding him shot after shot. As they laid him on the bed, they each took one side of him and started kissing all over him. One undid his belt to slide his pants off, while the other fed him another drink. Otis was so twisted he passed out. They took his wallet and car keys and left his drunk ass in the motel.

They went back to the hole in the wall to party some more and find their next prospects. Aunt Flo was on a mission to find this Danny guy so that they could get some more weed. It didn't take long for her to bump into him. Turns out Danny was looking for her too. He saw her dancing earlier and wanted to talk to her, but she left out before he could shoot his shot.

My aunt couldn't have cared less about Danny's interest in her until she found out he was a small-town hustler. He wasn't a real dope man because all he sold was weed, but he was caked up a little bit. Back then, everybody was smoking weed, and he had a nice size clientele. He told Aunt Flo what he could do for her. She took his number and told him that she might give him a call.

That night my aunt and Sheila had a real good time on somebody else's dime. The whole time they were in that hole in the wall, they didn't have to come out of their pockets to buy nothing. All those men were spending money on them. The guys would send them to the bar to buy drinks and then tell them to keep the change. They made bank that night and didn't get back home until like four or five in the morning.

Aunt Flo was nice enough to call the motel from the payphone to let Otis know where to pick up his car.

He was crying and begging, "Please don't take my money. My wife is gonna kill me."

Aunt Flo laughed and said, "You should've thought about that before you decided to play in the streets. You should've taken your old ass home with that money, square-assed-mutha-fucka."

It was a vicious game that she played with these niggas, but I liked it. Aunt Flo's mindset was they deserved it.

CHAPTER 8

WHERE YOUR LOYALTY LIES

Aunt Flo ended up calling Danny and hanging with him often. In Danny's mind, she was his woman, but to Aunt Flo, he was just her weed man. She used to go over to his house with Sheila. While she ran distraction on Danny, Sheila was in the back, robbing him blind. They did this for about five months. He knew what they were doing, but he liked my aunt so much that he allowed her to rob him of his weed.

One day, Aunt Flo and my mom were sitting around bored and decided they wanted to get high. Neither of them had money for weed, and Aunt Flo couldn't get in contact with Sheila. So, she decided to include my mom in her plan instead.

She said to my mom, "I know where we can get some weed, but you have to follow my lead."

Aunt Flo schooled my mom on who Danny was and what he did.

She said, "All you need to do is talk to him for five minutes while I go in the back to get the score."

Aunt Flo knew it was best for her to go in the back

because she knew where his stash was and could take as much as she pleased.

At the time, my aunt was two months away from turning eighteen, and my mom was already twenty-one. Danny, on the other hand, was thirty-two, and he liked young girls. So, my mom was the perfect exchange for Aunt Flo while she copped weed and money from Danny's stash.

They got to Danny's spot, and Aunt Flo introduced my mom.

She said, "Danny, this is my sister Patricia."

Danny looked my mother over, checking her out.

He gently grabbed her hand and said, "Hey Patricia."

Aunt Flo said, "Well, y'all get to know each other. I gotta go to the bathroom."

As Aunt Flo disappeared to the back, Danny got busy trying to make his move on my mom to get into her young draws. My grandmother would say, if you wanted to get a piece of my mom, all you had to do is bop her on the head, and her legs would fly open. That's how easy it was. I think my mom just wanted to feel loved and admired, but she just went about it all wrong, which always caused her to end up hurt.

My mom was smitten by Danny. She totally forgot she was supposed to be helping my aunt run game. The only problem was he really wanted Aunt Flo. I'm sure my mom knew that, but she still exchanged numbers with him. She eagerly developed a sick friendship with him that was built on him priming my mother with questions about Aunt Flo.

Couldn't she see that he really didn't want her? Couldn't she see that he was using her to find out what my aunt was doing? Couldn't she see that she was just a piece of ass to him? I mean, even I could see that, and I was just nine years old at the time.

Danny would call my aunt's number, and I would answer the phone.

"Hello."

He'd say, "Let me speak to Flo."

I'd say, "Flo's not home."

Then he would hang up and call my mother's line, and I would run to answer her phone. They lived in the same house, so how stupid was that? One day he called my mom's line.

I answered, and after he asked for my mom, I said, "Hey Danny! This is Danny, right?"

I could tell that he was taken aback by the fact I had figured out that he was calling both lines asking for my aunt and my mom. As he stumbled over his words, he threw up a lie.

He said, "I'm not Danny. My name is Kevin."

I just laughed and laughed.

In my mind, I said, "Fool, you got caught, and I'm going to tell."

I was a mischievous but smart child.

I'll never forget that hot summer day when it all came out. Aunt Flo found out that my mom was dropping dime on her to Danny. My mom would tell him every time my aunt left the house and who she left with. The icing on the cake was when my aunt caught my mom running around the corner to meet Danny.

I'm not sure what tipped Aunt Flo off, but she followed my mom as she left the house that day. My mom went over to the next street and hopped in the car with Danny. Aunt Flo watched as my mother kissed Danny, and that's when she made her move. She rolled up to the passenger side window and tapped. My mother looked like a deer caught in headlights.

Aunt Flo smirked and said, "Hi, you're busted!"

Of course, they tried to explain their way out of it. Aunt Flo didn't care that my mom was seeing Danny because it was all a game to her. What made her upset was that my mom didn't show any loyalty to her. She betrayed Aunt Flo by telling this man all of Aunt Flo's business. Unfortunately, this was the first of a long list of betrayals to come. As it turned out, my mother had no loyalty when it came to her family period, not even her kids.

It was like this man had her stupefied. She was mesmerized by his pimp game and his swollen tongue of lies. She pretty much worshipped him and constantly put him before herself, her kids, and her family. For example, she would feed her children hotdogs and beans, and it'd be the cheap hotdogs at that. You know, the ones that were $0.69 a pack and tasted like fake plastic chicken. So, while we ate the nastiest hotdogs in America, she'd serve Danny steak and salad like she worked for some fancy steakhouse waiting on him hand and foot. Again, that was only the beginning.

I remember one time my grandparents and Aunt Flo left town to go visit relatives in North Carolina. My mom told us that she also was going out of town for the weekend and that Uncle Bruce would be watching us while she was gone. That night, my mom packed a bag, then she put us to bed, acting like she was going to leave the house. I laid there with my eyes closed, pretending to be asleep. I secretly watched as she put her naughty nighties in her little bag of tricks, then left to go into my aunt's room.

I just assumed she went in there to get something, but then I heard a knock at the front door. I couldn't see who it was, but I heard my mother introduce her guest to Uncle Bruce as Kevin. I recognized that voice and the fake name, and I knew that treachery was afoot. The way my bed was positioned, I could see down the hall, and I saw my mom and Danny go into my aunt's room together. They were some trifling asses!

All I could think about was if I told my aunt, she would probably kill my mother. Like I said, I might have been a child, but I was a very smart child. They said I was too grown but look at all this stuff I had to deal with. There was nothing but grown shit all around me.

How could any woman screw her sister's man in her sister's room, in her sister's bed, in the house where your whole family lives, and all while your children were in the next room? You even paid one of your brothers to watch your kids and cover for you! What the Fuck? That just made me mad. I hated being lied to. It felt like she put a nigga before her kids once again. I was hoping and praying that my grandparents would come home and catch her.

The next morning, I went to my aunt's door and started knocking. Uncle Bruce came up to me in the hall.

He said, "Get away from that damn door! You always doing shit!"

I said, "We're hungry, and I want my mom to fix us some breakfast."

He said, "Your mama's not here. She went out of town."

I replied, "Yes, she is. She's in there with Kevin!"

"Get your ass away from that door! I'll fix y'all some breakfast," he said, irritated.

That day, my uncle let us go outside. It was the first day me and my sisters were allowed to go outside and out of the yard. He didn't really want to watch us. So, I decided to press our luck.

I asked, "Can we go to the rec center?"

Without even looking at me, he said, "Yes, but keep your eye on your sisters."

I enjoyed the rec center. I got some books from something called the bookmobile. It was the first time I'd ever seen a bookmobile. It was like a portable library inside of an RV. Just like a library, you could go into the bookmobile and check out books to read. It was awesome!

That day at the bookmobile was the spark of something beautiful. I discovered a love for reading, and those books were a great escape from life. I would get lost in the stories and pages of the books I read. Fantasizing and writing stories of my own would later become a place of sanctuary for me when life wasn't as kind. I guess now I understand why my mom loved her romance novels so much.

When we got home from the rec center, Uncle Bruce fed us and put us to bed early. My sisters kept asking him when our mom would be back.

He said, "I don't know, maybe sometime tomorrow."

I said, "You're lying. She never went nowhere. Mommy is here."

My sisters excitedly said, "Mommy is here! Mommy is here!"

Raising his voice, Uncle Bruce said, "Stop getting them all riled up. Your mother is not here!"

I said, "Yes, she is! She's right back there in auntie's room."

"Take your grown ass to sleep, little girl," Uncle Bruce said as he turned off the lights and closed the door on his way out of the room.

My sisters were disappointed, and I was simply annoyed by the lies, but we all went to sleep anyway.

Around 11 p.m., we were abruptly woken by a huge commotion. I could hear my grandparents' voices coming from the other room. My sisters and I jumped up and opened the door to find my granddaddy pushing and pounding on the door to my aunt's room. Finally, he kicked the door open just in time to see the tail end of Danny climbing out the window.

My granddaddy pulled out his pistol and ran to the window. He let off two shots—pow, pow. The chain-fence rattled as Danny jumped over it. He took off running through the alley with his shoes and shirt in his hands. My granddaddy stuck his head out the window.

"Did I get you?" he hollered.

Danny didn't look back. He just kept running.

Granddaddy pulled his head back in and shut the window. He gave my mother a look of pure disgust.

He said, "What are you doing, working on number four?"

My mother snapped back, "I'm grown, and you can't tell me what to do no more."

My granddaddy said, "Lies you tell, not in my house! I'm not going to have no whoremongering here!"

They argued for hours. I thought Granddaddy was going to backhand my mother right in the mouth. He was known for slapping the shit out of somebody. If any of his children raised their voice or argued with him, he would backhand the shit out of them. He didn't care if you were four or forty; raising your voice at him was a sign of great disrespect. My mother must've forgotten. She was yelling and screaming at the top of her lungs that she was an adult.

Finally, my grandma said, "If you think you grown, then get your ass out of here. Go out there in them streets, and let's see how grown you really are."

My mom came back in the room and gathered us up.

"Come on," she said.

I asked, "Mom, where are we going?"

"Don't worry about it, just come on," she said as she yanked up the small bag of clothes she had thrown together.

My mom made us walk for what seemed like forever to my aunt Julie's house. It was pitch black outside, and the only light came from the headlights of the cars going by. My sisters and I were complaining and whining the whole way. I was crying because I didn't want to leave my grandparents' house.

I thought to myself, "How did it get like this? When did the tension start?"

Then my mind went back a few months to my 10th birthday.

My cousin Belinda, who lived across the street from my grandmother, was my playmate growing up. It was my birthday, and she'd asked my grandparents if we could have a party in the backyard. Belinda knew that my mom treated me different from my sisters. She thought it was unfair the way my mom would dote over my two sisters and not me. So, she wanted me to have a birthday party to help me feel special on my big day.

My grandparents were fine with the idea but told me I'd have to run it by mom. I didn't think it would be a problem since it was Friday, and we didn't have school the next day. Belinda and I ran to my mom for permission.

Without hesitation, she said, "No."

I said, "Ok."

Belinda tried to console me as I sat on the porch and cried.

Granddaddy came out of the house and said, "Girl, what is wrong with you? Why aren't you getting ready for your party?"

Belinda said, "We ain't having a party, Granddaddy. Patricia said no."

He replied, "What are you talking about? Y'all go back there and clean up the yard for your party."

We didn't ask any questions and started cleaning up and decorating. Meanwhile, Granddaddy went to my mom.

He said, "Patricia, let me talk to you for a second."

"Daddy, I don't have time right now. I have a date to get ready for," she said.

"A date? Didn't them kids ask you if they could have a party in the backyard?"

"Yeah, Daddy, but I ain't got time to entertain that. I got plans."

Granddaddy said, "Hold up right there. This child doesn't ask you for nothing. She gets straight A's all through the school year, and you can't let her have a party for her 10th birthday? You give the other ones a party. Hell, you just gave Veronica a party, and you won't give this child one? You gonna bust hell wide open! If you don't change the shit you doing to that child, you gonna be sorry."

My mother paid him no mind. She just kept getting ready for her date.

Granddaddy turned to her and said, "Give me $20."

He knew she'd just got paid earlier that day.

Oblivious to why he was asking, she said, "What you need it for, Daddy?"

Granddaddy held out his hand and said, "Don't worry about that. Just give me the money."

My mother gave him the $20.

"I'll give this back to you when I get my check," he said.

"Ok, whatever, Daddy," she said as she continued getting ready for her date.

My granddaddy left my mom and went to my grandmother.

He said, "Helen, I need you to make a cake for Blu's birthday."

My grandmother looked at him and said, "Now? Walter, I don't feel like cooking no damn cake. It's 4 o'clock."

He said, "Will you just do it for me? Please, Helen."

Grandma shook her head and said, "Well, if you going to get me the stuff for the cake, then you better be going."

Granddaddy went to the store and bought some junk food for the party. He called the neighbor who worked at the grocery store and asked her to bring him a meat tray for my party when she came home from work. Then he asked Belinda's brother, Petey, who was a self-proclaimed DJ, to DJ the party. Granddaddy was calling in all the favors and pulling out all the stops. I had no idea all of this was about to go down. I thought it was going to be me and my friends eating chips in the backyard.

My mom left the house around 6 p.m. and didn't even say bye. After she left, I went in the house and got dressed. She didn't know about my party, and I sure as hell wasn't gonna tell her. About an hour or so later, Belinda came back to the house with Petey, and he bought his turntable. That's when I realized it was gonna be more than just juice and chips.

It was gonna be a blowout. We were getting ready to turn this mother out! All my close friends chipped in, hanging up lights and setting out chairs. I felt so special. This was my first "adult-like" party, and it turned into what seemed like a block party. Even older kids came. Since Petey was the DJ, all his friends came too.

My little birthday party put me on the map and made

me well known around the neighborhood. Kids that didn't know me certainly learned who I was that day. Even the ones that didn't like me wanted to be my friend now. We partied until midnight. Granddaddy had to pull the plug on it.

He told everyone, "Ok, four hours is enough time to play. Time to shut it down."

That night when I went to bed, I felt like I was the queen of the world. My granddaddy really made me feel special.

The next morning when my mom came home, she wasn't happy.

She came to me and said, "Didn't I tell you that you couldn't have a party? And you went behind my back and asked your granddaddy anyway? I was going to take you and your sisters to the movies, but now I'm not taking you nowhere since you already had your party."

Granddaddy heard my mom and came in the room.

He said, "Patricia, you know good, and damn well you wasn't taking them kids nowhere. Stop trying to make her feel bad. If you cared anything about your daughter, your ass wouldn't have been flapping in the wind last night! You would have been home doing something with these girls."

That made my mother really mad, and she felt some kind of way. Her attitude started to change again, and things started getting real tense around the house. Now we're here with no place to live.

When we got to aunt Julie's house, my mom told her version of the story. She bent the truth and told a lie. Aunt Julie let us stay with her for a few days until my mom was able to find a place for us to live. Aunt Julie really cared about my mom. Maybe it was because my mom babysat for her years ago, or maybe it was because of me.

Aunt Julie did a lot for me. I often felt she looked out for me because she knew her brother, Dee, was no good and wasn't doing right by me. Don't get me wrong, he and my mom were both kids when they had me. They didn't know nothing about taking care of a kid, but he didn't try to learn nothing either, not at seventeen anyway.

CHAPTER 9

OUT THE FRYING PAN AND INTO THE FIRE

Once again, we had moved out of my grandmother's house and into our own apartment. My sisters and I had a room to ourselves, which was an upgrade from us all living in one room at my grandmother's house. Our happiness was short-lived. Not even two weeks later, Danny, aka Kevin, aka the dirty-ass old man that had my mother hypnotized, moved in with us.

There was something wrong with that picture, though. When you have a stranger move in with a single mother of three little girls, that is a recipe for calamity, misfortune, and tragedy. The way my mom introduced us to him was like she served him up on the lid of a trash can and expected us to eat it up. It was bitter going down and bitter coming out. It all boiled down to a "crock of shit."

Mom said, "I want to introduce you guys to my friend."

I already knew his sorry ass. He was the man my granddaddy shot at, and he was the reason I had to leave my grandparents' house.

Danny looked at us and said, "Hi, nice meeting you guys. I brought a treat for you!"

He reached behind his back and pulled out three little bags of barbecue potato chips. Now he knew good and well ain't nobody eatin' no damn barbecue potato chips. Where was the salt & vinegar chips? I guess we should have been grateful.

I said, "Thank you, Kevin."

He said, "No, little girl, my name is Danny. Who's Kevin?"

I said, "Mhmm."

We took them sorry-ass potato chips from him, and then my mom sent us to our room.

Next thing we knew, Danny was all moved in like he owned the place. He went from staying overnight to living with us. My mom treated that nigga like he was the king of the roost, and he treated my mom like shit. He didn't start off treating her like that, but I was always told that it's not how you start; it's how you finish.

I was in the fourth grade and had just transferred to a new school. Danny had stayed out all night. My mother was angry getting up that day, just as she was angry going to bed the night before. This particular morning, she asked me to fix my sisters and myself a bowl of cereal for breakfast before school. I went to fix the bowl of cereal, and when I opened the milk, a sour smell came out of it.

"Oh, my goodness! This milk is spoiled. I'm not eating this," I said to my sisters.

They responded, "We're not eating it either."

They went back into the room and told my mom that they were hungry. She came running in the kitchen with a red leather belt wrapped around her knuckles, with about eleven inches of the end with the buckle hanging down.

She screamed at me, "Didn't I tell you to fix them some cereal?"

I said, "Yes, but the milk is spoiled, and I'm not eating it."

She said, "It's your fault that your sisters are not eating. You are the ringleader. You're always starting something."

She started hitting me with the belt. I held up my arm to protect my face and my upper body because she was hitting me sporadically all over like a wild woman. I felt like her personal punching bag. She needed to get her aggression out on somebody. Unfortunately, that morning that somebody was me.

My arms were welted and bruised all over, and parts of my arm were swollen. I went to school with my eyes full of tears. The tracks from my tears still stained my face as I walked into class, quietly sat down, and started my classwork.

Each morning we had a morning warm-up to do on the blackboard that was our morning classwork. I wept softly because my arms were still very tender from the whipping that I endured earlier that morning. My teacher came over to the desk.

She touched my arm and asked, "Are you ok?"

I cringed from the pain when she touched me. She rolled my sleeve back and saw the welts. Immediately she took me, this poor little black girl with tears in her eyes and looking all disheveled, to the nurse's office, and they brought in the counselor. It seemed like the administrators and the principal, who were all white by the way, were waiting for a good child abuse case. They could hardly wait to call Child Protective Services.

CPS interviewed me and then called my sisters into the office to talk with them. All three of us told them the same story about what happened. The funny thing about it is, when you are telling the truth, it's always the same story. It's nothing practiced, nothing rehearsed or coerced.

When they contacted my mother, it was the beginning of my punishment. They did an extensive investigation on my mother, her dope-selling-old-ass-boyfriend, and how she let this man she barely knew move in with her three little girls. She lied and told them he didn't live there and that he just spent the night sometimes.

Danny was a manipulator, and my mother was a liar. My mother lied to other people and herself. Like the day Danny came home with an infant boy in his arms. He told my mother that that was his son. The baby wasn't even two months old. Now, most women would have thrown that diaper bag around his neck and then told him to get the hell out, but not my mom. She was a real sucker. She was oohing and aahing, talking bout "He so cute."

In reality, the child looked like a newborn baby rat. He was a preemie. Now, it takes nine months for a baby to develop; and if this child was premature, this nigga was messing around on my mom. Why couldn't my mother figure that out?

Instead of her saying, "You hit the skids with this kid," she relished the thought of having a son and embraced the situation of this man messing around and having a kid on her. I couldn't get mad at the child and blame him. After a while, he grew on me, and I embraced him as a little brother.

Anyway, CPS continued interviewing and investigating the alleged child abuse situation. My mother bent the truth and told a lie like she often did to make herself look like the victim in all of this. She said that I was a hard-headed and unruly child that was spoiled and just wanted to live with my grandparents. That really wasn't the case at all. Like I said, whenever she got upset with her makeshift boyfriend, she would take it out on us girls, us meaning me.

I heard the phrase, "It's your fault that I was a mother at the age of fourteen," a lot. Instead of being honest and blaming her out of control hormones, skipping school, hooking up with guys, and her being a "fast ass," my mother blamed me. But wait, she was also a mother at seventeen for the second time and a mother again at nineteen for the third time, but I never heard her say anything like that to my sisters. I guess I was the first bad egg to start the ball rolling. At least that's what she wanted me to think.

My mother coerced my sisters into changing their stories and telling CPS that they made everything up. They also said I had told them to lie. My sisters were afraid of my mother, so it wasn't that hard to persuade them. How could I have told my sisters to lie? I didn't even know CPS was going to them.

In the end, Social Services, with my mother's approval, decided that I would take part in weekly counseling sessions with the school guidance counselor. I was labeled a problematic and troubled child because of the lie my sisters were forced to tell. I wasn't mad at them, though. They were afraid of what my mother would do to them. They were afraid of being beaten and punished like I so often was.

Things only seemed to get worse as even my sisters started to believe that I was a problem child—half the time, I was getting punished for them. My own sisters, who I looked out for and tried to protect, turned on me.

The following year we moved to Garden apartments in Maryland, which was a rough development. We were supposed to be moving on up like The Jeffersons, but it seemed more like James and Florida Evans—barely keeping our heads above water. This was around the time that crack became the hottest drug on the street. Danny, the supposed hustler and self-made man found himself getting high on his own supply. I swear the first rule of drug dealing was don't get high on your own shit.

High, or not, that man influenced my mother in ways you wouldn't believe. It started with small things like food. She would go to the store to buy snacks for the house. She'd buy only one box of snack cakes for me and my sisters to share but buy him boxes of his snack of choice. Our snacks were gone in two or three days, and we were told not to touch his food. Now, if we're all living in the same house together, doesn't that make it all our food?

Sometimes Danny would come home in the wee hours of the morning and tell my mother to wash his clothes. My mother would wake me up to go down to a dark laundry room to wash this man's clothes. I was just eleven years old, and she was sending me out the house by myself at sometimes three in the morning. It was dangerous and scary. People would be down in the laundry room smoking crack and having sex. I could have gotten attacked or even raped at that time of night. All sorts of things of that nature happened during those days in urban developments.

As time moved forward, Danny didn't get any better. He started staying home from work more and more, which caused us to move often. It seemed like we jumped from school to school, and it was hard making new friends. As soon as I made a friend, I had to move. I felt so alone. My mother chose a man over her daughters, and I felt like she didn't love us anymore. I had to stand up and protect myself and my sisters because we didn't have our mother as our protector anymore.

Getting through elementary school like this was bad enough, but it got worse when I started Junior High School. I found out that Danny's daughter, Tasha, was starting the same Junior High as me. I already felt awkward and inadequate, and now I had to deal with this.

My mother said, "If you run into Tasha, don't mention anything about Danny living with us."

I didn't understand why, but I followed my mother's instructions. Ironically, Tasha had every class with me, even homeroom. How jacked up was that?

She came to school with nice clothes, nice hairstyles, and nice jewelry. She bragged about all the things her father and mother did for her, which I found hard to believe since he was living with us, barely working, and using the drugs that he was supposed to be selling. It was my old faithful mother, the workhorse, helping him pay his child support so his child could be taken care of while her own children went without. Actually, I went without the most because Michael paid child support every now and then for my sisters.

My mom would say to me, "I'm taking your sisters shopping because their father gave them money. Your father ain't gave me shit for you."

Was that my fault too? Was I supposed to go fill out the paperwork to make my father pay child support for me? She's the one that neglected to file on my behalf. It was hard trying to compete with the other kids with the discount store specials I had to wear. I couldn't get as much as my sisters got because I was bigger than they were.

My mother said, "Since your clothes cost more, you're only getting two outfits."

My sisters were smaller, and they would start off the school year with five outfits apiece. I, on the other hand, had to start off with two pairs of pants and three tops.

This was hard for me to go through. I felt worthless and trapped in life. The kids in school teased me about my clothes and how I looked because I was a big girl. When they teased me about my size, it made me mad. I became more and more aggressive each day.

Tasha was in with the "it girls," and me and my friends were the "whatever girls." Now, the "it girls" were the girls whose parents had a little money. They got their hair done every two weeks, wore nice clothes and jewelry, and thought they were cute. The "whatever girls" responded, "Whatever," to the "it girls" boastings of, "Oh, I got this, and I got that."

One day, Tasha came to class wearing this brand-new pair of shell top Adidas bragging about what her father bought her. When I came into class with my new Reebok look-alikes from the discount store, all the kids started joning on me, asking if they were the new Reeboks. They teased and laughed at me for days. Every time I walked through the halls, they laughed and pointed at me.

My friend, Ruby, who was in another class, heard about what happened to me from the other kids. She was tired of them teasing me, especially Tasha. Ruby got so mad she let the cat out of the bag. She told everyone in our gym class that Tasha's father lived with my family and that my mother was the one taking care of him because he was strung out on drugs and hardly went to work. She even told them that the times that I missed school was not because I was sick but it was because I had to stay home to watch Tasha's little brother.

Of course, it didn't take any time for this juicy piece of

gossip to spread through to our other classes. Tasha got wind of it and decided to approach me:

She asked, "Is it true?"

I told her, "Yeah, it's true!"

They could not believe it.

Some kids asked, "If it's true, why do you look like you look? You come to school with Aerobics, and she's wearing Adidas."

Tears welled up in my eyes as I responded, "Because my mother is paying Tasha's Daddy's child support to keep him out of jail. She is taking from us to give to you, Tasha."

The whole class let out a resounding, "Ooh."

Tasha turned around and said, "Your momma ain't nothing but a lying Bitch."

That's when I punched her dead in her face. I tried to make my fist a permanent part of her eye socket. I kept aiming for her eyes and nose. As her body went clamoring into the lockers, I could hear the oohs and ahhs of the crowd. I felt strong. I was no longer a weak little girl. This was the last time those kids were going to tease me without any blowback.

The vice-principal came to break up the fight. Tasha was crying because I kept telling her this wasn't over. I even threatened to ride her bus home from school to beat her up again. I was sent to the guidance counselor's office, and eventually, they contacted our parents.

When I got home, I knew I was in for it. I got a whooping for fighting and was punished for a week. Tasha's mother had contacted Danny, so he went over to their house. When he got there, he saw that Tasha had a black eye. So, when he came home, he wanted to whoop me again.

My mother told him, "No. I've already beat her ass and punished her for a week."

He said, "Well, then add another week for running her damn mouth."

I didn't mind. It felt good finally being able to sock it to Tasha, although I wished it had been her father instead.

I was always punished for some reason or another. My aunt Flo heard about what happened and called the house to check on me. Danny answered the phone.

She said, "Can I speak to Blu?"

He said, "No," and hung up the phone.

Aunt Flo called back, and again Danny answered the phone.

She said, "Excuse me, can I speak to Blu? I'd like to speak to my niece, please."

He said, "No, she's punished," and hung the phone up again.

Anyone who knew anything about Aunt Flo knew she had a bad and short temper, especially when it came to being nice or patient with someone she couldn't stand. She decided she would call one more time before she'd show up on our doorstep to confront Danny's disrespectful ass. What really got her goat and made her show up after the third call was when she called back and made it known that it was her calling.

Danny said, "I don't care who this is. She's punished," and hung up on Aunt Flo for the third and final time.

Aunt Flo's fuse was lit, and she was ready to blow. She looked at my grandparents, who had been sitting there watching all of this unfold.

She said, "Ughh!!! He hung up on me again! I'm going over there because something ain't right. They won't even put her on the phone."

My grandmother said, "Yeah, Patricia said that Blu was punished. She can't even use the phone to call us."

My granddaddy jumped in and said, "That is some bullshit. Flo, you go over there and find out what's really going on. I want to know why Blu is punished for so long. What are they doing to her over there?"

My granddaddy never liked Danny and sure as hell never liked that my mother let him move in with us. My granddaddy was an old country boy, and back in his day, they didn't shack up.

My granddaddy used to say, "A woman will do more for her boyfriend than she'll do for her husband."

That was a saying I wouldn't understand until I became an adult. If you don't know what it means, I'll explain it to you later.

Aunt Flo was steaming mad when she jumped in her car and left my grandparent's house. She stopped to pick up her ride or die, Shelia and headed to my mom's house. When they arrived, they were ready to beat the brakes off Danny's slow ass.

Aunt Flo knocked on the door, and Danny went to answer it. She immediately got indignant with him.

She said, "What did you say on the phone motherfucker?" as she pulled out the billy club she had tucked in the back of her shirt.

Danny couldn't muster a word as he stared at my aunt in shock.

She pushed past Danny and continued, "Where is my niece? And don't you tell me I can't talk to her!"

My mother ran out of her room to see what was going on.

Aunt Flo, confused, said, "Patricia, you were home this

whole time, and you let this motherfucker keep hanging the phone up when I called to speak to Blu?"

My mom said, "Well, Flo, Blu is punished."

Aunt Flo looked my mother up and down and said, "So what does that mean to me?"

My mom quickly replied, "Oh, absolutely nothing because you're her aunt, and she can talk to you."

My mother wasn't a fighter at all. She must have thought about what would happen next if she answered wrong. The next thing I knew, my mother was yelling my name.

She said, "Blu, come out here and hurry up."

I came out to find Aunt Flo standing there. I was so happy to see her. I thought she was coming to get me and take me away with her.

Aunt Flo said, "Blu come here. I want to talk to you."

She took me out on the porch away from my mom and Danny.

She said, "Are you ok? Your grandma and Granddaddy wanted to make sure you're alright over here."

I sighed and said, "Tell them no, I'm not."

I went on to explain to her what happened and why I was punished.

Aunt Flo said, "I don't care what Danny says, no matter what, you call your grandparents every day so that they can know you're alright. And for the record, this punishment is bullshit. You should've whipped her ass. I ought to go in there and punch Patricia in the eye for even putting you on punishment."

I laughed softly, but I wanted my aunt to do just that. I know it was wrong of me to feel that way towards my mom.

I said, "Well, at least you could bust Danny upside his

head a couple of times since he made you use up your gas to come over here."

She said, "It only took five dollars."

I thought to myself, "They should take five dollars off his ass."

The thought tickled me so much I laughed wholeheartedly out loud.

Aunt Flo said, "What's so funny?"

I shook my head and said, "Nothing. I'm just happy to see you. Oh, why were you calling for me?"

Aunt Flo paused a moment in thought.

She said, "Oh damn, they made me so mad I forgot. Anyway, let me be on my way."

I gave her a hug and a kiss and prepared to go back in the house.

As Aunt Flo started to walk away, she turned and said, "Remember what I told you. Every day, you hear?"

I said, "Yes, ma'am."

Of course, my mother and Danny were lurking, trying to figure out what Aunt Flo and I were talking about. I couldn't even get all the way in the door before the questions started.

My mom asked, "So what did she want with you?"

Shrugging my shoulders, "I don't know, she never said."

Danny said to my mother, "You know she's lying. She ran all up in here for nothing?"

My mom said, "I know she's lying." Rolling her eyes at me, she continued, "Take your lying ass and get back in your room!"

I started walking to my room.

Then my mother yelled, "You're still punished, and I should punish you for another week just for lying."

I didn't say a word. I hung my head, went in my room, and got my clothes ready for school the next day.

I said to myself, "One of these days, they're going to push me too far, and I'm going to fuck both of them up."

I went to school the next day, but Tasha wasn't there. After all that trash she had talked, she was too embarrassed to show her face with a black eye.

The crazy thing was now that I'd laid an ass whooping on Tasha, every day that week, somebody was testing me. I felt like a gladiator in the ring—always ready for the next contender. At the same time, a lot of people started feeling differently about me now that the truth was out about Danny and where Tasha's money for fly clothes came from. I wasn't some little bum bitch anymore. I was now the victim of unfortunate circumstances. Everybody knew Danny as a piece of shit and thought my mother was crazy to be with him and put up with his mess.

Soon after, I became one of the cool kids. Why? I don't know. Maybe it was because I was a scrapper. I would fight boys and girls; it didn't matter. I was fighting to get my respect. I found myself fighting almost every week, but I never got suspended.

The guidance counselor saw that the hostility I had was a direct result of my home life. My teachers felt sorry for me because they knew I was a good student. I got straight A's, but every time Tasha looked my way, I wanted to punch her in the face.

It went on like this until school ended for summer break. Ironically, Tasha had to come to stay with my family because her mother got a boyfriend that wanted to tell Tasha what to do—just like her daddy did us.

I was blown away the day Danny decreed, "There will be no other man disciplining my children."

Well, well, well ain't that something. So, if no other man could discipline his kids, why was he always trying to discipline us?

When Tasha came, they treated her like she was the Queen of the Nile. They even let her go into the living room and sit on the furniture, which was forbidden for me and my sisters to do. Nevertheless, I tried to bury the hatchet and befriend her instead of burying my fist in her face.

I said to her, "So, what's your story? Why are you here?"

She said, "I had company over while my mom was out like I always did. My mom's boyfriend is always in my business trying to tell me what to do, but I ain't having it. So, now I'm here."

I'm not sure if the man hit Tasha or not. All I know is Danny ran out of here that day saying he had to go get his child.

After a few weeks, Danny talked to Tasha's mother. She came to her senses and let Tasha come back home. The following school year, when we went back for eighth grade, she treated me different. She no longer acted like she was better than me. We were equal.

CHAPTER 10

CALL OF THE WILD

The summer before the eighth grade, my personality started to shift. After constantly hearing I was a terrible child, I decided to emulate that. I started acting out and had a major attitude. I was flirtatious with older boys and invited people over to my apartment when my mother and Danny weren't home. At this point, I felt like I had nothing to lose. I felt like I was trapped in that house, in that life, in that abuse.

I remember one time I was cleaning up my mother's room, and under the TV was a Tupperware dish full of marijuana. I knew that the marijuana belonged to Danny, but I didn't know whether he was selling or smoking it. Either way, I didn't care. I hated him so much I took the marijuana and flushed it down the toilet.

Temperatures continued to heat up between Danny and me. He felt I was going against everything he would do, and I was because I knew it wasn't right. He even told my mother to get rid of me.

He said, "Blu is the cause of all of our troubles. You need to get rid of her. Send her ass back to your parents."

I wasn't the problem, though. Danny was doing drugs and unable to keep a steady job, but he blamed me for all their problems. Can you believe that?

My mother bought into it. She was convinced that it was me and that I was the root of all evil. The next morning, she was in the yellow pages looking for foster homes. I could hear her on the phone describing me. The first place she called told her I was too old, and since I hadn't done anything, they couldn't take me. Then they gave her another number to call.

As I sat listening to my mom call different foster homes, I wondered what was going to happen. My own mother was trying to get rid of me. She preferred to send me to live with strangers rather than let my grandparents come to get me. What were these strangers going to do to me? I would rather be dead than be raped or beaten by strangers in a group home. I was already getting abused enough as it was.

Danny had some pills in a jar hidden in the back of the refrigerator. He claimed they were diet pills, but I'm pretty sure they weren't. They were black capsules and known as black beauties on the street. The next day I took twelve black beauties, one for each year of my life that had passed, then went to lie down. My sisters saw what I did and were crying.

I was asleep when my mom came home from work. She came and started beating me because I was supposed to be watching my little sisters. I was so high; I didn't feel a thing. My sisters told my mother what I did, and she called the ambulance. Then she called my father. Funny how she knew my father's number all of a sudden.

How is it that she's calling him now? She never called him for child support, never called him when I needed school clothes, never called him when I was sick, but she was calling him now. Little did I know, this was part of her and Danny's plan to get rid of me. I was to be shipped off to my no-good-daddy, but that wasn't revealed until later.

By the time my father showed up at the hospital, my granddaddy was there too. My mother had told my grandparents what had happened. I think she was scared of what they would do when child protective services got involved. Danny was still poising the pot.

He told my mother, "Blu is just spoiled, and this is nothing more than her trying to get attention."

My father said, "Well, where did she get the pills from?"

Not only did my father want to know that answer, but the police did too. Turns out I was right. They weren't diet pills. They were speed. That's why they were called Black Beauties on the street.

I should have told them I found the pills nesting safely beside the milk in the back of our refrigerator and that the pills belonged to Danny, I didn't. Instead, I lied to the police and told them I found the bottle on the way home. I purposely failed to mention where they came from because I was afraid my mother might go to jail. Maybe if I had told on her, it would have woken her up; but being young and having a caring heart, I said nothing.

I spent several days at the county hospital's psych ward on suicide watch. When I came home, I was punished, of course. They made my mother take me to see a psychiatrist, but nothing came of the few visits I had with her. When the therapist told my mother Danny should not be there with us girls in the household, my mom concluded I was just spoiled and that the therapist did not know what she was talking about. My mother terminated my sessions before I even got a chance to tell my story.

So, now my mom decided to bring my father into the

fold. Why? I don't know. It's not like I was going to actually listen to him. He was a total stranger to me. I remember when my father showed up on my mother's doorstep. He stood with a belt behind his back, calling himself trying to discipline me.

My mom was like, "Surprise! Since you want to be disrespectful to Danny, get bad grades, smoke weed, have sex, and drink, I called your daddy to come whoop you."

According to my mom and Danny, I was doing everything under the sun. But it was all lies. Danny made up all of that so they could call my father to "discipline" me.

I said to my dad, "I'm a straight A student. How can I be skipping school and still be a straight A student? The only time I missed school was to watch little Danny. And I don't care what they say; you're not touching me with that belt."

My father began swinging the belt, and I started swinging my fists. We fell to the floor, but I kept hitting and kicking him. I was not going to let this man lay his hands on me, at least not without fighting back. Danny sat at the dining room table, looking at us wrestle in the living room like it was some type of show. My father had suffered a back injury from an accident on his job. Our wrestling match further aggregated his injury. I didn't feel bad for my father further injuring his back. I felt that he got what he deserved.

Eventually, he couldn't take the pain from his back, and we were finally able to calm down and talk. I showed him my accolades, my report cards with my high GPA, and my achievement awards. I even showed him where I was on the principal's list.

I asked him, "Now, how could I do all the things they accused me of and keep my grades up?"

My dad apologized and agreed that the problem wasn't

me. He told me he would talk to my mother and tell her the same. I don't know whether he ever talked to my mother or not, but the mere mention of him made her angry.

As soon as you'd say his name, she'd say, "He ain't shit!"

She claimed she didn't know that he would come over there and try to whoop me. It didn't matter, though. After that beating from my father, I stopped caring. I stopped trying to be a good girl. I made the decision to be even worse than before. Being good came with too much pain and hurt, and nobody cared about me anyway. There were perks to being bad. People respected and noticed you.

I admit I was mischievous at times and boy crazy too, but what thirteen-year-old wasn't at that time?

Ruby and her family lived across the court from my house. Her family was really into the church. I even went with them sometimes, but that had nothing on our love for boys.

Often, I was the go-between for Ruby and the guys she liked. There were a lot of guys that liked her too, but that was mostly because of one thing--to get in her pants. Once they got that one thing, they moved right along. Ruby would use me to pass messages to the ones she really liked.

I would go to the guy and say, "My friend over there is trying to get with you, so what's up?"

There was this one boy named Eric Shane. He was tall, bow-legged, and light-skinned with light brown eyes. He was cute, and all the girls wanted him. I was a tom-boy, so I was cool with all the boys. I thought he looked at me as a buddy, but I found out later that he liked me more than just a friend. He often caught the bus over our way to see Ruby.

Ruby wasn't allowed to have male company. Her mother thought she was too young to court. In fact, her mother said we had no business messing with these boys. So, Ruby asked if she could come kick it with him at my house when nobody was home. She wanted to be alone with Eric so she could get her freak on. Ruby was my home-girl, but she was a freak body. I knew I wasn't supposed to have company when my mom wasn't home, but Ruby talked me into helping her.

So, after we came home from school, Ruby and Eric came over to the house. We were sitting in the living room watching TV when Danny came walking through the door early.

He yelled at them, "Get the hell out of my house!"

He tried to make a scene but only set himself up to get jumped. He kept screaming and cussing at Ruby and Eric, but all of that was unnecessary.

Danny went to his room and got this thick leather belt, and when he came back, he swung it at me. I grabbed the end of it and wrapped it around my arm. He told me to let it go, but I didn't. So, he punched me in my chest. I fell back onto the couch. He charged at me to hit me again, but I leaned back and kicked him in his stomach. You would've thought we were in the Matrix by the way he went flying into the wall. I ran to my room, and he came in behind me.

When he came at me, I fell on the bed and started bicycle kicking him in his chest and stomach. I maneuvered to stand up, and he started punching me. We were fighting like two grown men, and I honestly don't remember how it ended. I just remember Ruby and Eric were gone, and my mom came home jumping on me about the fight with Danny.

She screamed, "YOU THINK YOU BAD BECAUSE

YOU'RE FIGHTING AN ADULT! IF YOU'RE SO BAD, FIGHT ME!"

She knew I would never raise my hand to hit her. She kept pushing me until I was backed into the corner with no escape. Looking back, maybe I should have knocked the shit out of her. Maybe that's who I should have been fighting instead of Danny.

As my mother was scolding me in the corner, Danny reached over my mother's shoulder and punched me with a right hook that landed on my left jaw, causing my head to hit the wall. It literally knocked the taste out of my mouth. I was dazed but somehow managed to shake it off. I pushed my mother out of the way, ready to get the hell out of there.

Danny tried to block my path, so I ran around the dining room table and bolted out the front door. I ran as fast as I could to Ruby's house. By the time I got there, my face had already started swelling. Ruby's mother looked at my face and was horrified. My face was swollen, my lip was busted, and my nose was bleeding.

Ruby's mom said, "Is there someone I can call to come help you?"

I said, "Yes, my grandparents."

She immediately called my grandparents and told them to come quick because I had been beaten badly.

She told them, "I don't care what she did; they had no right to beat her like this."

I stayed at Ruby's house until my grandparents arrived. When they saw my face, they were mad as hell, and my granddaddy wanted to kill Danny.

My granddaddy said, "Where that nigga at? He wants to beat on little girls, do he?"

My granddaddy had his pistol in his pocket and was ready to go take Danny out.

My grandmother, still in shock, said, "Come here, baby. Let me look at you."

She looked at my face, then kissed and hugged me. Ruby's mom told my grandparents what had been going on.

She said, "Do you know Patricia, and that man keeps her out of school to take care of his son? And that ain't even the worst of it all. They keep her on punishment and ration out food to them girls like they're dogs. Sometimes she doesn't even eat."

My grandparents were appalled.

My grandmother asked me, "Why didn't you tell us what was going on?

I explained, "I wanted to tell you, but every time I speak up, my mom twists the story around to make it seem like I'm lying. Everybody believes her, and then things get even worse for me."

My granddaddy remained silent, but I could tell by the look on his face that he was filled with pure rage.

My grandparents took me back to my mother's house to get my things. My mother must have read her father's body language because she stopped him at the door.

She said, "You can't come in here, Daddy."

Anger burned within him, and a silent tear ran down his face as he and my mother stood staring each other down.

"Move, Patricia," my grandmother said.

My mother blocked that doorway like she was Danny's bodyguard or something.

My grandmother quietly said, "Calm down, Walter," as she pulled my granddaddy away from the doorway.

My granddaddy continued to stare at my mother as he

stepped away from the doorway. My grandmother stepped in front of my mother.

My grandmother said, "Now get out of the way so I can get this girl's things."

My mother reluctantly let me and my grandmother in.

My grandmother said, "Go get your things, Blu!"

She didn't have to tell me twice. I took off down the hall to go get my things, but I halted my steps when my mother started screaming at her.

My mother yelled, "You're not taking my children! Vicky and Veronica aren't going nowhere!"

My grandmother replied, "I don't want Vicky or Veronica! I just came for Blu."

Danny was sitting at the table with a smug look on his face. He had a bat in his hand under the table like he was waiting to ambush my grandparents. Little did he know my grandmother was three steps ahead of him. My grandmother had a switchblade concealed in her sleeve. Just as I turned to go to my room, Danny started screaming.

He yelled, "PATRICIA! PATRICIA! Come get your mother!"

I turned back around to see my grandmother had the switchblade up against Danny's neck.

My grandmother said, "Nigga, I ought to slit your throat. Who do you think you are?"

My mother didn't know what to do. She stood frozen, looking at my grandmother with the blade on Danny's neck. If she left the door, my granddaddy would come in, and she didn't want that either. My grandmother barked her orders to me louder this time.

"Blu, go get your things and get everything because you're not coming back here ever again," she yelled.

My sisters were standing in the room crying.

They said, "Blu, please don't go."

I said, "I'm not leaving you. I'm going to get help. I have to go because if I don't, they're going to kill me."

They looked at me and cried harder. It felt like my heart was being ripped out. I was so scared of what Danny would do to my sisters. I knew that I was the only thing stopping him from abusing them the way he abused me. I was fearful for Vicky the most because I saw the way he used to gawk at her. It was sickening. Even a blind person could see the lust in his eyes when he looked at her. He would do things to make her feel special and favored, then use her to tell him everything I was doing. I knew it would be just a matter of time before he started touching her.

After I got my things, my grandparents and I headed to the car. Danny's typical bitch ass came running out with the bat like he was ready to do something. My granddaddy pulled out his gun and pointed it at Danny.

Granddaddy said, "Stop right there."

Danny was no fool. He quickly ran his ass right back inside.

We drove straight to the police station to press charges.

The police officer looked at my face and asked, "Who did this to this child?"

My grandmother said, "Our daughter's boyfriend, Danny."

My grandparents went on and gave the police Danny's full name and address. The officers took pictures of my face and went over to my mother's house that night to arrest Danny.

We went to Family court and got a restraining order against Danny. He was ordered not to come within 50 feet of me. In the meantime, Danny took out a restraining order against my grandmother. Of course, my mother spun a different version of the story against my grandparents in support of Danny.

I was so sad and hurt that it had to come to this. It was like I couldn't stop crying. I cried all day and all night for days, so much so that my eyes swelled shut. I spent so much time crying I didn't even realize I had been saved.

CHAPTER 11

HOME AGAIN

Aunt Flo and her two kids, Cee-Cee and Crystal, also lived with my grandparents. We had a full house. My new room was going to be in the den, but my grandparents had been using it for storage. So, there was nowhere to sleep in there. So, I had to sleep in the bed with my aunt and her kids until they got a bed for me.

Aunt Flo had a queen size bed at the time, and my choices were to either sleep in the bed with them or on the floor with the roaches. My cousins were ages seven and four, and they peed the bed every night. I woke up smelling like piss every day. Even after I washed, I still smelled like piss. It was like my skin absorbed it or something. Some nights were so bad I just wanted to get out of the pissy bed and take my chances with the roaches. Instead, I would go to my grandparents' room and sit on the floor beside the bed and cry. I was so tired and wanted to get some rest.

One night while I was sitting in my grandparent's room weeping, my grandmother woke up screaming.

She said, "Oh no, Mama got me!"

Her mother had just died a few months prior, and she

was still heavy on my grandmother's mind. My grandmother thought I was her mother coming back from the grave to get her. She woke the whole house up. She was screaming, and I started screaming.

My granddaddy jumped out of his sleep and said, "What the hell is going on? Helen, did you lose your damn mind?"

Holding her chest, she said, "No, I thought mama came back and got me."

He stared at my grandmother and said, "Mhmm... What the hell you been doing to think your mama came back from the dead to get you?" He then looked down at me and said, "And why the hell you in here screaming?"

Sobbing, I said, "Because I'm tired of being peed on and smelling like piss."

That weekend my granddaddy sacrificed his lottery money and went out and got me a bed. I finally had my own room, and I felt like I belonged. No more going to school smelling like pee. I always felt safe and loved around my grandparents. Their actions always affirmed me.

At my grandparent's house, I was allowed to be a normal child. I had my own space and felt at peace. My grandparents gave me free rein in the house. I could sit wherever I wanted and eat at a table like regular people. My grandmother made me feel like I was loved and a blessing. I felt wanted there. I didn't get that with my mother or father.

My father was simply not there. He was living his life and didn't have time to be bothered with me. When I lived with my mom, I was constantly punished, taunted, and treated badly by her and her boyfriend. I was so restricted. My mom wouldn't let me sit on the furniture in the living room or dining room and made me stand while eating in the kitchen. I had no space of my own to retreat. I used to go sit in the closet to get some peace, but even that was a problem. My mother always made me feel like a burden and a mistake.

I was thirteen, and my eyes were constantly filled with tears. Like a broken record, I heard my mother blame me for her becoming a teenage mom and everything that went wrong in her life. I was haunted daily by the ultimatums Danny gave her to get rid of me. I lived my life walking on very thin eggshells with my mother when all I wanted was for her to pick me, love me, choose me.

Being back with my grandparents, my granddaddy made sure he reminded me that I was special, wanted, and not a mistake. With my grandparents, I never wanted to kill myself again. All my thoughts of suicide went away. All the time I lived with my mother, I felt unstable and wanted to die. That was not a normal state of mind for a child. I guess I couldn't wrap my mind around the thought of my mother not wanting me and loving me. Because of that, I had to go into therapy.

My ninth-grade school year, I went to Forest Park High School. I was supposed to go to the high school over where my grandparents lived, but they didn't have full custody of me at the time. So, I had to go to school where my mother lived. I couldn't and didn't want to go back to my mom's house because of the restraining order. So, I lived with my aunt Julie, who lived down the hill from my mother.

When the new school year started, I had to go to school wearing my grandmother's clothes. My mother refused to buy me school clothes, so I had no clothes for school. She was being a real bitch now that I wasn't living under her roof. I guess she called herself teaching me a lesson. She thought I couldn't make it without her.

I must admit, it was difficult being a young teen starting high school wearing my grandmother's sweaters, skirts, and church heels. No, it was terrible. On top of that, Ruby, who was supposed to go to the same school as me, moved to North Carolina, leaving me to start my first year of high school alone.

I didn't want to go to school, I was embarrassed! And I certainly didn't want to go without my best friend. I just threw myself into my schoolwork because that's the only thing I could do to keep myself from crying every day. It paid off because I found myself excelling at school—getting perfect scores on my assignments and acing every test.

My classmates started to take notice of my achievements as well. They warmed up to me, and as they got to know me, they found out that I wasn't afraid to speak out. Apparently, that is something that was admirable. It didn't take me long to make friends, and I had a lot of them, believe it or not. I guess it was my magnetic personality, or maybe it was the witty banter that I carried on with the kids. I don't know; it might've been because they knew I wasn't a joke.

"Don't fuck with her. She doesn't play," they would say.

It never stopped me from making new friends, though. But as much as they wanted to be my friend, I didn't want to be me. I wanted to be anyone but me because I didn't like myself. I knew I had to be careful with that kind of thinking because it could easily cause me to try to off myself again. Back then, I endured so much hurt and pain from my mom's rejection. I often felt I was better off dead than alive. To this day, I don't think I've ever gotten over that. I felt like a throw-away-child. That got damn mufuckin bish. How could she make me feel this way?

Tasha, Danny's daughter, remember that bitch? Well, we went to high school together, and she was up to the same old tricks. I thought she would've changed and grown up over the summer, but she was the same old snotty bitch. She was her mother's only child and always got what she wanted. It was a new set of "it girls," but the same old bitchy Tasha.

We had classes together, and she would tell people she didn't' like me—talking about I was poor and dirty, and my own mother didn't want to have nothing to do with me. When that got back to me, I was so enraged I was in kill mode. I knew that she had heard that from her father. How else would she know what went on in that house? I started the school year off, leaving that girl alone. I didn't even bother her, especially after what her father did. But after I heard what she was saying about me, I knew it was clobbering time.

All that practice I had from fighting her father gave me a wicked left hook. I stepped to her in the hallway.

All I remember saying to her was, "Did you?"

Before I could get the rest out, I punched her right in her eye socket.

As I punched her, I said in cadence, "Keep-My-Name-Out-Your-Mouth! Don't speak of my family business. It doesn't concern you."

This again would seem to establish me as a "bad person" or a part of the "bad crowd." But I wasn't. Every blow I hit her with was full of hurt, shame, and rejection. I don't know if I beat her because she said it or because I felt it was true.

Word got back to Danny and my mother, and they

brought it up in family court. They used it as an argument for why I shouldn't be around my sisters. They said that I was a bully, and my sisters were afraid of me, more lies, of course. Unsurprisingly, the restraining order was upheld, and I couldn't be around my sisters. There was still no decision on custody, so I remained at aunt Julie's and continued at Forest Park.

Even though attending Forest Park started off rough, the altercation with Tasha gained me the respect of my peers. I gained popularity for standing up for myself and was also known for standing up for other kids. So, beating her ass turned out to be a win after all.

CHAPTER 12

A NEW FRIEND

There was this new girl named Justice Hall that came to Forest Park. She was new to the area and to the school. She could have been an "it" girl, but she acted like a "whatever" girl. Other kids didn't like her because they said she thought she was cute. Justice was light-skinned, had long hair and green eyes. Little did they know her hair was a weave, and her eyes were contacts. Her sister Angel could afford to buy her all of that because they had money.

None of that made any difference to me or Justice. She was down to earth, and we immediately hit it off. It could've been because she was just as broken and damaged as I was inside. Her mother had died a few years prior from cancer. Her older sister, Angel, tried to take on the role of her mother and help their father raise Justice.

Every morning Justice would come to school with stacks of twenties in her pockets. Her sister's boyfriend was a big-time drug dealer, and they gave her whatever she wanted. That's why she could come to school with green eyes, hundreds of dollars worth of weave in her hair, and about another hundred in her pocket as milk money. Can I say I benefited from having a friend with some money? Let's just say I wasn't hungry.

Like me, Justice was super smart, and we became good friends. In ninth grade, we took the state functional test, and I got a perfect score. The staff was so proud to have a perfect score coming from their school. They announced it over the loudspeaker while I was in Mrs. Grey's English class. When they said my name, I was so embarrassed and just wanted to disappear. Once again, there was unwanted attention and yet another label on me. From that point on, I was a nerd. The kids made a big deal out of it, and of course, Tasha was mad. She started running her mouth again, but this time the kids shut her down.

They were like, "Girl, shut up, she could help you with your math homework. Shoot! I'd be her fake sister to get the grades!"

I became friends with people from the basketball and football teams. They were my homies and looked out for me, and I looked out for them with their schoolwork. That's not to say they were a bunch of dumb jocks, but they needed my help, and I didn't mind. The football team protected me, and I protected Justice. We had our own dynamic, and believe me; it came in handy.

Justice was liked by all the boys at school. We'd sit together every day during lunch, and there was always somebody trying to shoot their shot with her. I was like her bodyguard, especially when it came to guys she didn't like.

One day we were at lunch, and I sat my stuff down on the table and went to go get food for Justice and myself. When I came back, this guy named Lorenzo was sitting in my seat.

I put the trays on the table and said, "Would you kindly get the fuck out of my seat?"

He said, "Girl go sit somewhere else."

Then he took my tray and slid it to the other end of the table. I guess he must have pushed it too hard because it slid off the table and onto the floor. Everybody started laughing, but I didn't find any humor in it all.

I yelled, "Motherfucker!"

Lorenzo stood up. He was a tall, lanky dude, about 6'1. It didn't matter to me, though, because I knew I could take him with a couple of body punches. Sizing him up, I knew what I was going to take out first, his throat. While Lorenzo was cussing me out and telling me to take my ass somewhere else, I jumped on him. I punched him in his adam's apple, then he stumbled back four steps and fell.

"Timber," I said as I sat on him and started swinging.

I had to take him out before he got a chance to take me out. I realized he was a man and could have really hurt me if he had landed blows in the right places. Thankfully, he didn't.

The football team, who was eating lunch on the stage, saw what was going on and jumped off the stage to get me. After all, they couldn't have their tutor getting suspended, could they? They pulled me off Lorenzo.

Lorenzo got up and said, "Bitch! I'm gonna fuck you up!"

Two of the hottest football players stood in the middle of our crossfire and said, "Naw partner, I don't think so."

By this time, Justice was standing on the lunch table screaming and pointing at Lorenzo.

She said, "That's what you get! That's what you get, Lorenzo. You started it!"

The school administrator, Mr. Knox, came and said,

"Both of you are getting suspended. We don't tolerate fighting in the school."

Everybody started booing him. Then out of nowhere, a milk carton went flying in the air. Instantly, the cafeteria got real rowdy. The teachers started flicking the lights on and off to try to gain control, but that only made it worse. The second time the lights went out; food was flying from everywhere. Students were throwing food and fighting. The "it" girls were fighting the "whatever" girls, and it was a mess.

Me, Justice, and my cousin Tanya, who was a senior, slid out the side door because we knew the principal was getting ready to put the school on lockdown. When we got outside, we ran into this girl named Tiffany, who had already managed to slip out and was outside smoking. She invited us to come hang out at her house until the smoke had cleared and school was over.

When we got there, it was already a party kicking off because Tiffany's older brother Twon already had a few of his friends over. I pretty much kept quiet and observed since I didn't know the guys like that. Tanya, on the other hand, knew everybody and made herself right at home. We were all a bunch of pubescent adolescents smoking and drinking, so what do you think happened? With all their hormones raging, some of the people started to hook up.

One of Twon's friends walked over to Tiffany and started getting touchy-feely with her. Tiffany was either high as a kite or had lust in her eyes; either way, she looked like she was enjoying it. I peeped the vibe in the room, and it felt like me and Justice were being sized up. A couple of Twon's friends were staring at us, and it made me feel uncomfortable.

I turned to Justice and said, "Let's bounce! I'm not with this at all."

"OK. But it looks like Tanya wants to stay," she chuckled as she nudged her head Tanya's way.

I turned just in time to see Tanya leading one of the guys into a back room. I guess she was feeling old dude. Justice and I were the only freshmen there; everyone else was upperclassmen. Tanya was a "second time" senior and was five years older than I was. We decided to roll out without her. Besides, this shindig was more her speed anyway.

We left Tiffany's house and went back to Justice's house since nobody was home. I couldn't go back to where I was staying with Aunt Julie because she worked at night and was home during the day. There was no way I could tell her the trouble I'd gotten into at school, considering my situation. So, I stayed with Justice until it was my normal time to come home from school.

The next day, when we got to school, we found out that Mr. Knox had to be taken to the hospital because the kids jumped him and beat him badly. They broke his arm and his nose. The whole school was on an in-school suspension for three months. Mr. Knox didn't come back to school after that. I was scared they were going to say something to me and Justice, but they never addressed the fight with anyone after Mr. Knox got hurt.

Justice and I continued with life enjoying our friendship. One day while we were hanging out, this guy named A.J. called to me. Now, A.J. was a well-known hustler from around the way, and he was fine. A.J. always admired how Justice and I carried ourselves and did our thang. He knew we weren't the "it" girls and didn't care to be. We didn't go along to get along. We set our own styles and trends. If there was something going down that we didn't like, we would roll out quick.

A.J. said, "Come here, Blu. I got something I want you to do for me."

I put my hand on my hip and gave him the side-eye.

"UmmHmm, what could you possibly want me to do for you?" I asked.

He said, "I want you to pick up a package for me. Do you think you can do that?"

I said, "I don't know, A.J. What kind of package, and where am I going to pick it up from?"

A.J. laughed and shook his head. Then he plucked a $20 bill from the wad of money he pulled from his pocket and handed it to me.

He said, "Can you go around the corner to the carryout and pick up my food for me?"

"Oh! Is that it? I think I can manage that, no problem at all," I said.

"I'm afraid to ask you what you thought I would ask you to do," he replied.

I didn't bother to answer him.

Justice and I walked up the street and around the corner to get his food for him.

When we returned, I handed him his bag and his exact change. He looked at me as if I had two heads or something.

"What?" I said.

He said, "You're not gonna ask if you can keep the change?"

Confused, I said, "No, why would I?"

Kind of surprised, he said, "But you didn't even ask if you could get anything."

I waved him off and said, "It's no big deal, A.J. I needed something from the beauty supply store next door anyway. So, it didn't take me out of my way."

He said, "That's why I fucks with you! You are straight up, and I like dat about you. Where your man at?"

It was my turn to look at him like he had two heads.

I looked at Justice and thought to myself, "I know this dude ain't trying to get fresh with me."

I had the biggest smile on my face. I was cheesing like a mug because not only was he nice looking and dressed nice, but I had the biggest crush on him. But I had to play the role like I didn't care if he liked me or not. I acted as if I hardly ever paid attention to him and didn't care what he was talking about. In truth, I always did.

I laughed and said, "Oh my God, Justice check this. I know he's not trying to play me close."

Justice chuckled and said, "You know, I think he might be."

Smiling, A.J. said, "Y'all need to go head with y'all little fake gangster slang. Go pick up a book and learn something. But for real, Blu, I got this cat that I want you to meet. He's a real cool dude, and I think you would like him."

For a split second, I felt disappointed because he wasn't talking about himself.

He turned his attention to Justice and said, "And Justice, I got somebody that I want you to meet too," he said with excitement.

Justice said, "Uh, thank you but, no thank you. I've seen the kind of dudes that you hang with, and that's not even my style, cuz. I'm not interested."

"Alright, I can respect that," he said.

"I thought you would," she replied.

I chimed in, "Well, I'm single! I don't mind making new friends here and there, just as long as they are legit."

He said, "Word, I'm going to give my man Manny your number."

Frowning, I said, "Ewwwww A.J.! What kind of name is Manny?"

"See, I told you! Even this dude's name sounds like he's on some fuck shit," Justice said.

"She's right," I said with much attitude.

A.J. said, "Stop Trippin! Manny is short for Emmanuel."

"Oooh, I like the name Emmanuel," I said.

Justice agreed, "Yeah, that's cute."

"Nah, he sounds like he's on that fuck shit, remember," A.J. teased.

Justice and I laughed, then I said, "Go on and give him the digits."

Even though I had a crush on him, I allowed A.J. to play matchmaker and hook me up with his friend. A.J. was only four years older than us, but he treated us like his homegirls. He would look out for us from time to time and make sure no one was messing with us. I don't know who told him he was our bodyguards, but that's just how he ran things, and it was cool with me. I appreciated the extra love, and I knew that was his way of showing us love for real.

About a week went by before I got a phone call from Manny. He had such a sexy voice. It was like I was talking to the artist formerly known as Prince. Everyone who knew me knew that I loved me some Prince. Manny and I would talk every chance we got. I could not believe that I had so much in common with him. Not only did he like the same things that I liked, but he was smart in school, and he was a nerd just like me! He was also cool enough to hang around the in-crowd.

I was feeling me some Manny. If I had a type, he would

be it. Come to find out, we only lived a few blocks from each other. I often wondered how I had never met him before A.J. hooked us up. I could get to his house in about 10 minutes if I took the path behind the apartment building.

The path was cool and all, but it was only safe for daytime travel. After dark, I wouldn't dare go back there. I heard a lot of stories about how people would get raped, beat up, robbed, and even killed on that path behind the apartments. When the streetlights came on, that path was a big no-no for me.

Manny and I became really close over time. I enjoyed talking to him and was grateful that A.J. hooked us up. Over time Manny introduced me to some of his other friends, including Dawg and Psycho. Psycho's real name was Vincent, but everyone called him Psycho because he was a thug and didn't give a shit about nothing. He would do all kinds of wild off the wall things, not caring how crazy it was. Dawg, on the other hand, was pretty cool. He always looked me directly in my eyes whenever we spoke. Sometimes he would even stare and give me strange looks, but I often pretended not to notice.

Although Dawg gave me weird vibes, he was cool to me because he was always nice. I couldn't say the same about Psycho. The vibe he gave me was a totally different one. He literally made the hairs on the back of my neck stand up. I couldn't explain it, but his looks were sinister. It could have been the fact that everyone called him Psycho, and I was just being paranoid, but I highly doubted it. It was something familiar about him, but I couldn't seem to put my finger on it.

CHAPTER 13

JUSTICE BUT NO PEACE

The fight for custody of me finally was leaning in my favor. After all my mother and Danny's shenanigans, the court awarded my grandparents temporary full custody of me. It was great news, but this meant that I now had to transfer to Riverdale High School, which ultimately meant I had to leave Justice.

When Justice found out I was finally getting transferred to the school in my grandparents' district, she began to act out. She went ballistic on me as if we weren't even friends. I still had two weeks to finish at Forest Park before I could transfer to Riverdale. Well, in those two weeks, I saw a side of Justice that was unreal. It was almost like she was a whole different person.

She was depressed and didn't want to go to school there anymore. She ignored me in class and wouldn't walk with or talk to me while we were in school. This was so unlike her. I even caught her rolling her eyes at me a few times when she didn't think I was looking. She acted like she was one of the "it" girls.

She would converse and hang with people that

wouldn't even look twice at her on her best day. The ones I'd normally protect her from. They'd call her names like weirdo, loser, or nerd and wanted to beat her up because she was pretty. Now she hung with them like they were thick as thieves and as if I meant nothing to her.

Little did I know the pain I kept feeling in my back was just Justice stabbing me in it every chance she got. I found out she had been talking bad about me to the "it" girls, especially when she found out I was leaving. I guess she couldn't come and talk to me about her feelings like a normal friend would.

Then to add to her betrayal, she made up lies and seduced my friend named James. James and I liked each other, and Justice knew this. It pained me that she would stoop so low. James was sprung and would do anything for Justice. He went from talking to me every day to avoiding me like the plague.

He'd say things like, "Don't say shit to me bitch."

When I first heard the long list of insults come out of James' mouth, I was heartbroken. He and Justice went around the school spreading nasty rumors about me. One of the most hurtful rumors was that I gave him head in the boy's locker room during basketball practice. In actuality, I had never even kissed that boy! It was obvious that neither of them cared for me at all. But payback would be a bitch.

Turns out while James was falling in love with Justice, she was busy screwing two of his homeboys. In a matter of a couple of weeks, Justice slept her way through several people's boyfriends, including dirty Lorenzo, who got his name because he was always burning somebody. True to his reputation, he burned Justice too. He gave her Trichomonas, and she passed it on to everyone that she was sleeping with, including James.

That served his black ass right for sure. By the time I left for my new school, Justice had a nasty reputation as being a total slut bucket. She acted like that didn't even bother her, just like she acted like we were never friends. Of course, I was hurt. I didn't understand what I did to make her turn on me, but I couldn't dwell on it long. I just added her to the long list of people who disappointed me in life. Unfortunately, that wouldn't be the first or last time I'd get my heart broken by a "friend" that was more like family to me.

A few months had gone by when I got a call from Justice's sister Angel. To my surprise, she began to catch me up on all the things that had happened to Justice since I left. She told me Justice had come to her crying about losing her best friend, how much she loved me, and how I was like a sister to her. Then she told me Justice was in the hospital.

Angel explained, "Justice got jumped in the girl's locker room and was hurt really bad. She suffered a broken nose and cracked ribs. You should go see her. She could really use a friend right now."

I went up to the hospital immediately to see her. Despite all that had happened, she was still my friend, and I refused to turn my back on her or kick her when she was down. I wanted to show her how true friends treat one another and be by her side when she needed someone. But what Angel failed to tell me was that Justice was in the psych ward.

I didn't understand what was going on. I couldn't even bring myself to get on the elevator to go up to see her. I hopped on the payphone in the lobby and called Angel to make sure that I had the right information. I wanted to make sure they hadn't moved her without Angel knowing. My heart sank to my stomach when Angel confirmed it.

She said, "I didn't have the heart to tell you, and I

didn't want you to be scared away because she's in the psych ward. Blu, she didn't mean any of the things that she said or did to you. Honestly, I think that girl loves you more than me. Just go see her. She really needs you right now."

I was confused. If Justice loved me, why would she try to hurt me so bad? I know hurt people, hurt people, but what reaction was she looking for? It's not like I had a choice in the matter. Ironically, I had a choice now, and I decided I would do better by Justice than she did by me. Before hanging up with Angel, she had one more request for me.

She said, "Blu, once you finish your visit with her, call me. I'll explain everything else then."

I hung up the phone and built up enough courage to go upstairs to see Justice, but not before bawling my eyes out while sitting on the floor next to the payphone. I composed myself and took the elevator up to the 5th floor.

When I got off the elevator, I was greeted by a big heavy metal door meant to keep patients in and visitors out. Your name had to be on a special approved visitor's list to get buzzed in for visits. Angel must have known I would come because my name was in the book of approved visitors for Justice.

It was a madhouse on that floor. They had adults and teenagers on the same floor, but they were separated into different wings. There were all kinds of people in there— rich, poor, black, white, you name it, they were in there. I didn't know the severity of mental health until that day.

I walked into Justice's room as she sat staring out the window.

I said, "So, you did all of this just so I could come see you and bring you flowers, huh?"

I laughed out loud as she turned to see who had

entered. As soon as she saw me, she screamed with a loud squeal.

She said, "Blu! What are you doing here? I'm so glad to see you!"

I walked over to her and gave her a hug. Immediately she started apologizing to me.

She said, "I'm so sorry for the way I treated you. I said so many mean things to and about you that I really didn't mean."

I said, "Don't worry about that. Let's let the past be the past. Although I will admit, it hurt really bad."

Tears welled up in the corners of her eyes. Immediately I wished I hadn't said anything. It wasn't my intention to make her cry. So, I quickly changed the subject.

"So, when do you get to come home?" I asked.

She said, "In a couple of days, and then it will be like old times again. We'll be back in the same school, hanging out every day, and inseparable!"

Confused, I said, "Back in the same school? What are you talking about?"

She said, "Angel told me that you were transferring back to Forest Park, and honestly, I can't wait. I've missed you so much, and I'm tired of hanging with all those fake people."

Seeing Justice so happy and going on and on about us being back together was bittersweet. It was sweet to see that she missed me so much and still wanted to be my friend, but it pained me that it was all based on a fantasy.

I said, "It would be great for us to be back together again, but I can't come back to Forest Park. I've already started my new school, and now that my grandparents have custody of me, I can only go to school in their neighborhood."

Justice scoffed and said, "That's no problem. Angel will

pay for your tuition so that we can both go to private school together."

I said, "No, I don't want to go to private school. I actually like the school I go to now, and I don't want to leave any more of my friends and family behind."

At that moment, I noticed yet another shift in her demeanor. Justice let out this quirky snort-laugh then rolled her eyes like she used to do when she was in school. Her eyelashes fluttered as she rolled her eyeballs into her head, indicating I was getting on her nerves and irritating her. Then just like that, I was dealing with a different Justice. She had that same attitude she had when she turned her back on me.

Without warning, she said, "What are you doing here?"

It was as if she didn't remember asking me that, and her tone was much different. My antennas went up, and I began to pay close attention. She wasn't the same person she was just moments ago.

She said, "I don't even know why you came here, you dirty whore! You're not my friend. Everyone knows you're just like your mother spreading your legs for anybody and spreading all kinds of diseases. That's what you are; you're a disease! They told me everything you said about me behind my back."

I was floored and just sat there with my mouth open, fighting back the hurt and anger that was swelling up in me. I couldn't believe the things she said to me. She accused me of doing the very things she herself was doing. I knew she had lost touch with reality.

Without looking at me, she mumbled, "Leave!"

Still stunned, I sat and stared at her, confused.

Justice then yelled, "I said leave you dirty bitch! Get out my room!"

With tears in my eyes, I got up from the chair and headed to the door in disbelief. That's when she decided to turn the knife she just jabbed into my heart.

She said, "By the way, James and I are having a baby. But we'd never have our baby around a foul person like you."

I turned and said, "No matter what, just know I still love you. Keep your head up and please never stop taking your meds. Know that I'll always be here for you if you need me."

As I reached for the doorknob, she yelled, "It'll be a cold day in hell before I call you for anything, you slut!"

Without turning back, I said, "OK," and walked out.

I walked out crying, but I refused to let her see me cry. I was mad and hurt. I really didn't know what to think about her saying she was pregnant by James. Lord forgive me, but the only thing I could think was "that poor baby."

That evening when I got home, as promised, I called Angel.

Angel asked, "So, while you were with Justice, did you notice anything strange about her?"

I played dumb and said, "What you mean?"

She said, "You know when you were talking to her, did it seem like anything was wrong?"

I repeated, "If anything was wrong? A whole lot was wrong. One minute she was loving and acted like we were friends. Then as soon as she didn't get her way, she flipped out on me again, saying she never wanted to see me. She was a straight looney tune. Why didn't you warn me?"

Angel replied, "Blu, I needed you to see it for yourself. That other person was not the Justice we know. Justice is being evaluated for a personality disorder. She experiences these episodes where her thoughts and perceptions are disturbed, and she sometimes has difficulty understanding what's real and what isn't."

"What? How am I just hearing about this? I've been around her all this time and never seen any of this. I mean, I know she told me she got really depressed when her mom died, but nothing like this."

Angel interjected, "Let me stop you right there because that's what I'm talking about. Our mom isn't dead, Blu."

I said, "What? Justice has been telling me since I met her that her mom was dead."

Angel explained, "Our mom suffers from schizophrenia and is locked up as criminally insane. She tried to drown Justice in the bathtub when Justice was three years old. Dad finally had her committed when he realized she was a danger to herself and us."

I was stuck. I couldn't move, blink, or speak.

Angel went on to say, "I know this is a lot Blu, but it was easier for Justice to say mom died of cancer than to admit that she was schizophrenic and locked up for trying to kill her."

At this point, I wasn't sure if it was true or make-believe, but I decided to tell Angel about Justice saying she was pregnant.

Angel screamed, "WHAT!" She composed herself and then continued, "Thank you, Blu, but I gotta go. I'll talk to you later."

I didn't understand what she was thanking me for because I didn't do anything. The next couple of days, Justice was all I thought about. I felt sad for my friend, the girl I once called my sister. I couldn't imagine all she had been through and continued to deal with. She was trauma-tized, and my fear was she'd end up just like her mom.

About a week and a half went by before I heard from

Angel again. She once again thanked me for giving her that information and then confirmed that Justice was indeed pregnant.

She said, "The doctor's said Justice has something called manic depression. Her hormones being out of whack, coupled with her not taking her meds, is what caused her to go off the deep end. So, they're going to recalibrate her meds, and if she takes them regularly like she's supposed to, she will be fine. If you want, you can go see her."

"Thanks, but no thanks, Angel. I will wait until she's ready. She can reach out to me at that time. Just let her know that I will always be here for her. I don't want to add to her grief or depression."

Angel said, "I understand. Let me know if you change your mind."

"So, what's going to happen with the baby?" I asked.

She said, "We're going to keep it and have a talk with James and his family. Both of them laid down to make it so both of them should take care of it."

"I know James and his family personally. They're going to hit the roof when they get the news. His daddy is some big time judge, and his mother is an accountant at this prestigious law firm. They think they're all of that. I heard James had to beg to go to public school. I guess that's the lifestyle of the Rich and Shameless," I said.

She said, "That's fine, as long as the Shameless can come up with half."

We both laughed, even though the situation was as serious as a heart attack.

When Justice was around seven months pregnant, James' "rich to do parents" decided to do a DNA test. This is where money plays a big part. I didn't even know it was possible to have a DNA test done while the baby was still in the womb, but that is exactly what they did. James' parents were sure that James was not the father, and not just because he said he wasn't. See, they were told that Justice had slept with five other guys during the time she got pregnant. Therefore, his parents were adamant that without a test, they wouldn't be taking care of no baby.

I'm not sure how they pulled it off, but all the parents got together to have their sons tested. It turned out that James was not the baby's father after all. The biological father was none other than dirty Lorenzo. Guess who broke the news to me? Yep, James. He decided it was the best time to come to me and apologize and tell me how sorry he was. I didn't want to hear anything he had to say. He destroyed our friendship over a piece of ass. So, I told him about himself then offered him my ass to kiss.

I called Angel to tell her about James.

Panicked, Angel answered, "Hello!"

I said, "Girl..."

"Blu, I have to call you back," she said, then hung up the phone before I could say anything else.

I later found out Justice tried to commit suicide. When she found out Lorenzo was the father of her baby, she drank bleach, trying to kill her and the baby.

I was scared. Days had gone by, and I still hadn't heard anything from Angel. I didn't know whether to try calling their father or just wait. I decided to just pray for them, and in the middle of my prayers, Angel called.

She told me the baby went into distress, and they had to induce labor to save it. Justice gave birth to a baby boy.

Although they saved them both, the baby suffered brain damage from the bleach and stress. Lorenzo was by her side the entire time. He was in love with Justice, and he was happy to be her child's father, but Justice wanted to give the baby up for adoption.

In Justice fashion, she belittled Lorenzo and called the baby a little retarded monster. In the end, Lorenzo and his family decided to keep the baby with the understanding that Justice would sign over her rights. Turns out, Lorenzo was a trust fund baby. His grandfather left him one when he died. So, they were able to take care of the baby and provide for his needs.

I was thankful for Angel and how cool she was toward me. It felt like she was more of my friend than Justice. I heard through the grapevine that things continued to get worse with Justice. She went back to school, telling everyone her baby had died. The crazy thing about that was she and Lorenzo still went to the same school.

Of course, her lies backfired on her. People called her "little crazy," saying she was a baby killer. Justice sunk into that damn depression again, so Angel pulled her out of school and transferred her to a new school where she knew absolutely no one, giving Justice a much needed fresh start.

Chapter 14

HEAVY HITTER

Going to Riverdale was awesome. I made a lot of friends, and I felt popular. I played basketball and was the manager of the wrestling team. I got good grades and had a lot of upperclassmen as friends, whose respect I gained by fighting and standing up for myself.

All the kids from Palmer Park that I grew up with were there. I started elementary school in Palmer Park and left during the fifth grade leaving my cousins and friends behind. Reconnecting with everyone was great, and it was fun being around the old crew. I was especially happy to be back across the street from my cousin Belinda.

Belinda was now an "it" girl. I was a freshman, and she was a sophomore, and we caught the bus together every morning.

Belinda said, "The kids around here are ghetto as fuck. You gonna have to fight your way to get a seat on the bus. The boys bumrush the bus to get seated first, while all the girls stand back and wait for them to be seated."

What? I couldn't believe my ears. They didn't have no

fucking manners. It didn't matter to me what those other girls did. I wasn't about to be the last one on the bus, and neither was my cousin.

The very first day, when the bus pulled up, I grabbed Belinda's book bag and fought my way on the bus with the rest of those mutha fuckas. I was one of the first to get a seat and made sure that Belinda got a seat up front, right behind the bus driver. From that day on, it was established that I wasn't the one to be played with.

When I used to fight for my seat on the bus, I would go straight to the back where we clowned and had fun. One day after I had claimed my seat in the back of the bus, this girl Sonia Frederickson, came up to me.

She said, "You in my seat."

I said, "This is a public bus, and there are no assigned seats."

She said, "I said get up!"

Laughing, I said, "Girl, you better beat it."

She replied, "I'm gonna kick your ass, you fat bitch. I will see you later."

I said, "You could see me now, you crack head bitch! Go back and smoke your pipe!"

The whole bus went, "Ooooh."

Later that day, while we were changing classes, I had to make a pit stop at the bathroom. I was with my cousin Bobby, and he waited for me outside the girls' bathroom. Sonia and her two flunkies, Lakey and Michelle, were waiting to jump me in the bathroom. She knew she couldn't whoop my ass one on one, so she tried to pull her friends in on it.

Sonia was tall and skinny with a lot of mouth. She thought she was the baddest thing in Riverdale. She smoked weed and acted like she was a part of a motorcycle gang. She was the party girl. Michelle was tall, skinny, and dark-skinned with braces and long pretty hair. She thought she was the beauty queen of Palmer Park. Lakey was the cutest one. She was mixed with black and Chinese but had hair that stuck up all over her head. She was Sonia's lapdog and would do anything Sonia told her to do.

They were in there smoking when I stepped in the bathroom, but I didn't pay them any mind. I ran into the stall because I had to pee. When I came out of the stall, they were sitting on the sink, blocking me from washing my hands.

I said, "Excuse me."

Lakey said, "What was all that shit you was talking on the bus? Let's see if you can back it up."

I took that as a threat and punched her dead in her face. Pow! It was on. I turned to hit Sonia, and Lakey jumped on my back. I slammed my back against the wall to pin Lakey, and Sonia came at me from the front. Michelle tried to throw in kicks from the side.

Bobby heard the commotion and ran in the bathroom.

He yelled, "Get off of her," as he took his Spanish book and started giving them the smackdown like a wrestler with a chair.

The commotion could be heard outside in the hallway. Finally, the administrators came in and broke it up. They took us all to the principal's office. After we explained what happened, they let Bobby and I go. We were laughing because three girls waited to ambush me and instead got beat up. My reputation increased again because the baddest girls in school tried to jump me, and I whooped their asses. Sonia and her lackeys got suspended for three days.

Sonia's suspension was up a few days later, and she

returned to school. I took the back seat where I'd been sitting all week when the bus came.

All the other kids were like, "Oooh, here she come, here she come," as Sonia boarded the bus.

Sonia took the seat in front of me. She kept turning around, gritting on me.

Finally, she said, "You know this is not over?"

I said, "You damn right it ain't."

"Any time anywhere," she replied.

I went back to laughing and joking with my friends, but she just sat silently looking forward. I knew she had another ambush ready for me, but I didn't care.

Word got out around the school about what was "supposed" to happen when we got off the bus that afternoon. That alone prompted all these other kids, who didn't live in our neighborhood, to ride our bus home. They wanted to see the fight. Our bus was so crowded people were sitting on each other's laps to fit.

Just like on the way to school, Sonia sat in the seat in front of me. She turned, and I knew she was about to start talking shit.

Instead, she said, "Is Pea your sister?"

I said, "Pea, who?"

She said, "The one they call Sweet Pea."

I said, "Hell no, that's not my sister, that's my aunt."

She was referring to my aunt Flo. I'm thinking now, what does Aunt Flo have to do with this?

So, I said, "Why and what difference does it make?"

She said, "Oh, those are my folks, we cool like that. I can't fuck with you."

That didn't' make a difference to me. I was looking forward to an afternoon brawl, but Sonia bowed out.

She said, "Nah, you got it. Everything's cool."

When the bus got to our stop, there were two girls waiting for us to get off the bus. Sonia went to them, and I guess told them who I was, then everybody was all chummy-chummy. I was like, "whatever," and I walked home.

When I got home, I asked Aunt Flo if she knew Sonia Frederickson.

She said, "Yeah, I went to school with her sisters. Why?"

I said, "She was the girl that tried to jump me in the bathroom."

My aunt said, "Oh man, why didn't you tell me that she was the girl? I would have taken you around the corner, so you could've stomped her ass in the ground and dared her sisters to jump in."

Apparently, my aunt put enough fear in her sisters to last a lifetime because when they found out who I was, they didn't have any more beef with me.

My aunt and uncles were some heavy hitters. In gym class, the teacher saw my last name and asked me if I was kin to Bruce.

I said, "Yes, that's my uncle."

He said, "Man, I love that dude. Because of Bruce, we won the championship back in '79."

He proudly showed me my uncle's picture in the trophy case in the school lobby.

My aunt Flo and my uncle Bruce's reputation preceded me in high school. I had a legacy to protect, and I did not disappoint.

CHAPTER 15

WORKING GIRL

I had been living with my grandparents for about eight months when the time came for us to go to court so my grandparents could get permanent guardianship of me. When I saw my mother at court, it broke my heart all over again. I didn't want to live with my grandparents. I wanted to live with my mother and sisters without Danny.

As my mother sat there next to Danny, I couldn't believe how brainwashed she was by this man. Instead of her standing up for me, her own child, and her parents, she stood up for Danny and his lies. To this very day, I don't understand what my mother ever saw in him. The old folks always say, "beauty is in the eye of the beholder." Well, my mom had cataracts on her eyes because she couldn't see the ugliness of the shit Danny was doing.

I know my granddaddy's feelings were hurt to see his daughter put another man over him and throw her child to the side. He took it hard. That's why he and my grandmother came to my rescue.

He once told me, "As long as I'm living, I will never see any of my children or grandchildren end up in foster care. I never got rid of none of mine. So why should I get rid of any of theirs?"

Granddaddy believed in family, and for that, I am truly grateful.

The judge ruled and gave my grandparents custody of me. He also ordered that I go to therapy.

I said, "Your honor, I've been sent to counseling before."

The judge said, "Ok, so what happened?"

I said, "The therapist told my mom that she needed therapy too and that Danny was the problem. My mom didn't want to hear that and told them that I was just a spoiled brat that wanted my way."

If looks could kill, I would be dead because the look my mother gave me in that courtroom was like she wanted to do just that.

The judge said, "I see. Well, you'll be with your grandparents now, and I suspect counseling will do you more justice this time."

On my way home from court, I cried, and cried, and cried. I was happy to be with my grandparents and not be placed in foster care, but I was sad to be leaving my sisters behind. I told them I was going to get help for all of us, but it turned out to be help for just me.

I started working when I was thirteen years old. My first job was at Taco-Taco in Landover mall. My aunt forged my birth certificate to make it look like I was fourteen so I could be approved to work. I made $2.75 an hour.

I didn't want welfare benefits anymore. They were only giving me $150 a month. My grandmother would take $50 and give me the rest. I was a teenager, but $100 was not enough for me to live off for a month. I asked my grandmother to let me work and promised I would pay her $50 a month for rent. My grandmother agreed.

When I started working, I brought home an average of $75 a week, which worked out to be $300 a month. I was so excited when I got my first paycheck. I felt a sense of accomplishment and entitlement. Now I could contribute and help my grandparents take care of me. I felt they shouldn't have had to take care of me financially. That was my parents' responsibility, but neither of them wanted me at the time. I felt like I was a burden to my grandparents. Now that I was making my own money, it made me feel so much better.

I had my eye on a pair of white-on-white leather Nike tennis shoes. They were $39.99. Although I could have asked for them, I decided I would save up my money to buy them for myself. My first check was $77.00. I gave my granddaddy some money and saved the rest. When I got my second check, I went to Landover Mall with Belinda, and she bought me the pair of shoes I'd been eyeing.

When I put those shoes on, I felt really good.

Belinda said, "They look like boy's shoes."

My granddaddy said, "Blu, you paid way too much money for them."

In that moment, I didn't care what either of them thought about the shoes. I liked them, and I bought them myself. I felt on top of the world because I could buy myself things, and I no longer had to wear my grandmother's clothes.

I worked at Taco-Taco my whole ninth-grade year. Then I got an opportunity to go work at The Chicken Palace, which paid $3.50 an hour. When I went to The Chicken Palace for the interview, they hired me right on the spot. I was so happy – I got to work at my favorite place to eat in the world.

I never missed a day of work. I was there on time regardless of rain, sleet, or snow. My first big check was $117. I was moving up in the world, and working gave me a sense of self-worth.

I learned early in life that money is a game changer – it changes the way people look at you. That saying, "money don't matter," is a lie. With money, I could get my hair done twice a month and buy fancy clothes and shoes. I was keeping up with the Joneses, whoever they were. I looked good and had self-confidence.

I enjoyed working and making my own money. I enjoyed it so much that the summer before I turned sixteen, I managed to get two jobs. I worked the third shift at the Corner Store from eleven at night to seven in the morning. Then I came home and slept for a few hours before I headed to The Chicken Palace to work the mid-day shift. The money was good, and I really wanted to go to college. I knew I had the potential to become a doctor or something special. So, I figured this was a good way for me to save for my college fund.

I went to my grandmother and asked her to open a savings account for me. She told me to ask my mom. I didn't understand my grandmother's reasoning, but I followed her instructions and asked my mom. To my surprise, she was more than eager to help. She even invited me over to the house on the weekend, so I could spend time with my sisters. I should've questioned that, but I didn't.

Every other weekend when I was off, I'd go over there to visit with them. It just so happened to always be on my payday too. I would take my mom to get her hair done and do different things with my sisters, like take them out to eat or to the movies. I thought we were bonding and spending time together, but in reality, all I was doing was providing them with entertainment on the weekends.

My granddaddy would say to me, "You know you can't buy your mama's love?"

I would respond, "You're wrong, Granddaddy. I'm not trying to buy her love. I'm just trying to spend time with my mom and my sisters."

It always hurt me to my core when he would say that, but the truth is he wasn't wrong. I just didn't know it then.

Around this time, Danny went from selling dope to being a dopehead. He upgraded from selling and smoking weed to crack-rock and became one of the biggest rock monsters out there. He didn't heed the warning about not getting high on your own supply. He was his own biggest customer.

Again, what kind of a drug dealer was he for real? He had limited money and moved into a home with a woman and her three little kids relying on her to take care of him and his kids--kids that didn't even live with them. His habit put my mother in financial distress because she no longer had any help from this so called "drug dealer."

Danny would stay out all night and come home broke. Things became bumpy between them when he'd come up short on the rent. That meant my mother had to pay all the bills in the house, feed him, wash his clothes, and keep a roof over his head. That's in addition to doing all the same for my two little sisters. That didn't seem to bother my mother, at least not to the point she'd leave him. No, she still supported him and stood by his side through it all. Such a stupid, dumb fool!

What took the cake for me was when she gave him the rent money to buy a money order. That day Danny became a magician. Voila – poof! The money went up in smoke. Literally, he made that shit disappear. Do you think she kicked him out? Nope! She just cried and started borrowing money from her friends. She only managed to get half of the money she needed for the rent. That's when a light bulb must've gone off in her head, and she decided to take the money out of my account to make up the difference. She didn't ask, and I didn't even know she took it.

Correct me if I am wrong, but when somebody takes your money without asking, isn't that stealing? I didn't find out the money was missing until a week later when I made my biweekly deposit in the bank. I gave my granddaddy my normal deposit to put in my savings account and asked him to bring me a receipt with the balance. I wanted to see how well I was doing with saving my money.

Well, my granddaddy came back with the receipt. I was expecting to see something close to $800 after my deposit, but the receipt showed a balance of $105. I was shocked.

I said, "Granddaddy, something's not right."

So, my granddaddy and I decided to go back to the bank. We called my mother so she could go with us since her name was on the account too.

When I called her, I said, "Ma, someone stole my money out my bank account."

She sighed and then said, "Girl ain't nobody steal your money. I had something to take care of, so I borrowed it."

I said, "No, that's taking because borrowing is when you ask. My shit wasn't asked for. It was just snatched."

She said, "You heard what I said. I will pay you your little money back when I get it."

I wasn't trying to hear none of that. So, I just closed out my account. I was mad. That money was supposed to pay for my college education. She knew that, but she didn't care. I was just the throwaway child, and her needs always came first. That got-damn-mufuckin-bish was just using me. Once again, she made me feel as worthless as a used tampon.

CHAPTER 16

GRADUATION DAY: GROW THE F*CK UP

My mother robbing me of my hard-earned money didn't keep me down. I just got back on my grind and worked double to recoup what I'd lost. That summer, I made sure I worked two jobs. I had no life! While everybody else was partying and having fun, I was working. All I had was my work and my writing.

Writing kept me sane. I would have sunk into a depression if it wasn't for my love of writing. I felt like everything I had was taken away from me. After I worked so hard to make straight A's, I wasn't even going to graduate with the rest of my class. When I transferred from one high school to the other, some of my records were lost, leaving me with missing credits--credits for classes that I had already taken and passed with an A.

When I went to the guidance counselor to plead my case, she said, "All you have to do is go back to your old high school and get the transcripts."

Now by "you," she meant my guardians, which was my grandparents. So, I went to my grandmother.

Her response was, "Blu, I'm too old for all this. I don't

want to be running from school to school trying to fill out paperwork. Ask your mother to do it since she lives over there by the school."

Of course, that was like a fart in the wind. She wasn't going to help nobody, but I went to her anyway because my grandmother told me to go ask her.

You would've thought my mom would have been like, "Sure, I'll get those papers for you so that you can graduate on time with honors." Nope.

She said, "Ask your grandmother. She's your mother now."

I was so hurt. I didn't know what to do. I asked my cousins, Belinda and Bobby, who were a part of my graduating class, for advice, but they didn't have any for me. I even talked it over with Manny, who was more like a boyfriend to me, except we didn't do anything but talk all the time.

He said, "Do whatever will make you happy. I'll support you with whatever you decide."

So, I came up with an idea, and I went to tell Belinda and Bobby.

I told them, "I've decided to quit school."

They started crying like babies. They knew I aspired and dreamed of going to college to become a doctor.

I went on and said, "Stop crying and let me finish. I have a plan. I'm going to drop out of school and go get my GED."

Back then, if you dropped out of school after you turned sixteen years old, you could wait a few months then take the GED test. So, my plan was to drop out and get my GED. This way, I could still get into a junior college and later transfer to a four-year university.

Belinda asked, "You can't try to get the transcript on your own?"

I said, "I tried, but the school said I needed to have a parent or guardian to sign the paperwork, and I don't have a willing parent or guardian to do that for me. So, I'm taking matters into my own hands."

Me getting my GED was the only way I could see out at the time. So, that's what I did. I went to the office at my high school and told them I quit. My guidance counselor was flabbergasted. She had high hopes for me. I'm sure she thought I let my situation get the best of me, but I didn't. I made the best of a bad situation.

When I told my grandmother what I did, it didn't seem to bother her at all. She came from that generation where getting a job was more important than getting an education. But we weren't in the '50s and '60s anymore. We were in the '80s. For you to make it in this world, you needed an education. Although a good education wasn't important to my grandmother, it was to my granddaddy.

He said to me, "I never had a chance to go to school because I had to work the farm."

That option was taken away from him, but he wanted it to be different for me. It hurt Granddaddy to his heart to hear I was dropping out. He felt that because I was working, I wasn't going to go back to school and pursue my dreams. I knew I had to show him otherwise, and that's just what I did. I continued working while taking the GED prep classes. Then I took the test and got my GED.

I thought Granddaddy would have been happy that I got it, but when I told him, he still seemed sad. I understood why. I felt sad too. I would have been the first one in our family to graduate and walk across the stage. None of his children walked across the stage; all of them got GEDs. It made me sad to know that I couldn't do that for my granddaddy, and it wasn't even my fault.

I worked so hard to be an honor student, and when it came time for me to shine, I couldn't. All because of some missing documents that these grown-ass adults could've easily gone and signed. That just gave me one more reason to resent my mother. She took so much from me, and now my graduation too. I didn't understand why this lady had so much bitterness in her heart for me. I guess I will never know. All I knew was it was time for me to grow the fuck up. So, I continued working hard to save money for college.

On my 18th birthday, I decided it was time for me to move out.

My grandmother said, "When you turn eighteen, you can do whatever you want."

While living with my grandparents, I wasn't allowed to date boys or go out, but I could work all day and all night. So, I had a list of all the things I planned to do once I turned eighteen, and moving out was at the top of that list. Well, it was after I got punished on my 18th birthday for staying out all night. That was the catalyst that propelled it to the top of the list.

I decided to hang out with my cousin Tanya to celebrate my 18th birthday. She was a wild one that liked to go out to clubs and party. Her favorite clubs were gay and African clubs, but she enjoyed any club where there was music, a fully stocked bar, and a good crowd. My grandparents warned me about hanging out with her.

They said, "Tanya is too wild for you, Blu."

On my 18th birthday, I said to myself, "I'm going out, fuck it!"

I wanted to cut up and see what life was about. I remember it like it was yesterday. I wanted to do something different for my birthday since I would be a grown woman. So, I called Tanya.

Slightly winded, Tanya answered, "Hello?"

I said, "Hey Tanya, what's up?"

"Nothing much, just sitting here talking to one of my friends," she replied.

I said, "Which ones?"

She said quickly, "You don't know them!"

"Why do you sound like you're out of breath?" I asked.

She laughed, "Why do you ask so many questions?"

Laughing, I said, "I'm just making small talk. You know my birthday is next weekend, right?"

"Girl, I can't forget my favorite cousin's birthday! What do you have planned?" she asked.

"I really don't have anything planned yet. I'm trying to make plans now."

She said, "Well, what do you want to do, Blu?"

I thought about it and said, "It would be nice to get away from the house and hang out."

Excited, she said, "Say no more! I know just the place, honey. We're going to a club, so make sure you wear something cute! You're about to be grown, so I don't want no push back from you. All I want you to worry about is what you're going to wear, and make sure your ass is ready to go no later than 6:30."

Ok was all I could say, and with that, we ended the call.

My cousin took me to this African club, where we drank

and partied all night long. I didn't get in until 5 a.m. the next morning. Not only had I stayed out all night long, but I was hanging out with wild ass Tanya. So, there was no telling what I was doing. At least, that is how my grandmother saw it.

I walked into the house happy because I had just had the time of my life. It felt good to be eighteen because I had never been able to do what I wanted to do before.

"I could get used to this," I thought.

I was shocked to see my grandmother was still up when I walked in.

"Where have you been, and what were you out there doing at 5 a.m. in the morning, huh?" she shouted.

I said, "I went out to a club with Tanya. It was great! The club was so much fun, Grandma. There was food, music, and drinks. The people were so nice to me. They kept offering me things, but I didn't take any pills or smoke anything. The only thing I did was drink a little champagne because it was my birthday."

She said, "Well, how did that make you feel?"

I said, "I didn't really enjoy the champagne. It was nasty, and it gave me a slight headache, but I'm not sure if that was from the loud music or the champagne."

"Did that make you feel like an adult?" she asked.

"I feel the same, just a little tired," I replied.

WHAP! Without warning, she slammed the belt that I didn't realize she was holding on the table. I was scared she was going to whip me.

Panicked, I asked, "What did I do?"

She said, "You stayed out all night long!"

I said, "But you said when I turned eighteen, I could do whatever I wanted."

She quickly responded, "Not in my house! As long as

you live in my house and are under my roof, you have to do what I say! YOU'RE PUNISHED!

Confused, I said, "Punished?"

She said, "That's right Punished! You can't leave this house for two weeks unless it's to go to work."

As grown as I thought I was, she quickly reminded me how much I wasn't, even at eighteen. I felt stupid and dumb. The happiness was quickly sucked right out of me. Here I am practically grown, and my grandmother is punishing me. I was out of school, worked two jobs, paid rent, and paid for my own phone line! Hell, I even had my own beeper. It felt like she was punishing her tenant.

Later that day, I told Tanya what had happened.

I explained, "I won't be able to hang out again until I'm off punishment."

Tanya said, "That is ridiculous! You know you can always move in with me, right? I think it will be a good idea, Blu! Besides, my roommate is no longer here."

"Okay! I'll do it," I said.

She asked, "Do you think you can pay your half of the rent now?"

I said, "I'm not moving in until I'm off of punishment, which is two weeks away."

She said, "I was hoping you would move in sooner because I kinda need the rent money now."

I thought about it and said, "Sure, but I'm still moving in when I get off of punishment at the beginning of the month."

"Okay, that will be your first month's rent," she said.

It was pretty much a done deal. Tanya had convinced me to move in with her. Now that I think about it, I think she just needed me to pay half the bills since her previous roommate had recently moved out. In my mind, it was the perfect opportunity. I thought it would give me a chance to gain freedom and grow up. I wanted to feel like I was responsible and on my own. But I had enough respect for my grandmother to wait until after I finished my punishment to move out.

Tell me, how many people do you know that would wait until they finished their punishment to move? Most would say fuck that shit and move out right then and there. Not me; I didn't want to disappoint her. I loved her so much, and like a rescue dog, I owed my grandparents my life.

The next day when Granddaddy picked me up from work, I decided to break the news to him.

I said, "Guess what, Granddaddy?"

"Chicken butt," he said.

"I found a place and will be moving out," I said.

He said, "Blu, where are you moving? You can't afford to pay rent by yourself, so who are you moving with?"

As he fired off questions, I could tell he was concerned.

"Tanya," I said.

He exclaimed, "Tanya! You mean wild ass, Tanya? Hmph, if you do, you're a stupid dumb fool! She ain't doing nothing but trying to use you because that's all she does is use people."

I sat there and just looked at him. I was trying to read his expression to see if he was just saying that to make me change my mind or if he really believed she was using me. I just couldn't tell what his angle was. He must have been reading my mind because before I could say anything, he interrupted.

He said, "Trust me, Blu, moving in with her would be a big mistake."

"Aww, Granddaddy, I honestly didn't want to hear

anything else because my mind was already made up. I was looking forward to moving out," I said.

He scoffed, "Alright! You just don't believe shit stinks until you stir it, huh, Blu? I done told you over and over again what her real name is, and you never seem to listen. Her first name is NOTHING, her middle name is BUT, and her last name is TROUBLE."

I said, "Granddaddy, you always say that."

He said, "And I'm always gonna say it too. A leopard doesn't change its spots, you know?"

"I know. I just feel like everybody gives her such a bad rep," I said.

"Trust me; she does that all by herself. Did you tell your grandmother yet?" he asked.

I said, "Nope, I thought you would mention it to her."

He belted out, "Like hell, I will! You're grown, remember? You will have to tell her yourself."

I said, "Okay, I will."

The rest of the ride home was silent. I'm not sure what Granddaddy was thinking about, but I was thinking about my freedom and how everybody always threw salt on Tanya. Her own sister, Kia, would even refer to her as a "crazy tri-polar bitch." I never understood the term, but then I figured it was only because Tanya had such a free spirit and would try anything. Honestly, that is what lured me into feeling it was a good idea to live with her. I knew she cared about me, and her being a free spirit sounded like a good thing.

When we got home, I went straight to my room. Granddaddy, on the other hand, sat at the table with my grandmother.

I heard him say, "Helen, Blu got something to tell you."

Loudly my grandmother said, "What is it, Blu? What you got to tell me?"

I came out of my room and sat at the table with them so I could see my grandmother's face.

I said, "Well, I found a place, and I'm moving out."

She said, "Girl, you talking nonsense. You can't afford a place by yourself."

I said, "I know! That's why I'm not moving by myself. I'm moving in with Tanya."

She scoffed, "Hmph! Fine. Well, I hope you can stay out there on your own because you ain't coming back here!"

I knew she was trying to scare me into staying.

I replied, "Okay."

"When are you moving?" she asked.

I said, "In about a week and a half, on the first of the month."

Every day for the next week and a half, my grandmother asked me the same questions when I got home from work.

She'd say, "Blu, are you hungry? Did you pack yet?"

In that same amount of time, she also taught me how to budget and what I needed to do to have my phone service transferred to my new address. Although I didn't have much to move, I made sure my granddad was free to help me move my things. The apartment already had a dresser in it. So, all I needed to move was my bed and some clothes. I was all set!

The day before move-in day came rather quickly. I was so excited. I decided to call Tanya to let her know I was all packed and ready. I wanted her to know I would be there early the next morning and needed to make sure that she'd be home to let me in. When I called, her phone just rang busy. I figured I'd just try again in the morning. That night I was too excited to fall asleep. I was thinking about the money I was able to save and making a mental note of the things I wanted to get for my place.

I decided to give Manny a call, and he picked up on the first ring.

He answered, "Hello."

I said, "Dang, how'd you manage to answer so fast?"

He chuckled, "I was laying next to the phone. What's up?"

"Nothing, I just can't sleep. You know tomorrow's the big day."

He said, "Yes, I am so excited for us."

"Us?" I asked.

He explained, "Yeah, with you having your own spot and all, I figured me and the guys would have a place to kick it."

Now, Manny had technically been my boyfriend since I was sixteen and working at Taco-Taco. We weren't sexually active or anything, but we did have a few taboo conversations over the phone. We talked about any and everything, and I liked him a lot. He claimed he was a virgin, but I wasn't naïve. I know guys will say whatever they think you want to hear.

"Oh no! I'll be working most of the time, so it won't be like that," I replied.

I had just started working for a new company called The Uniform Place on the swing shift from 3-11 p.m. I'd given up my two part-time jobs for the one full-time that paid more than both put together. There was no way I was messing up my money hanging out.

He said, "Ok, we'll see."

Manny and I ended up talking on the phone for a few hours. We decided to call it a night after he caught me drifting off a few times.

The next morning, I woke up to the smell of breakfast. I'm not sure what my grandmother was feeling at that moment, but she had pulled out all the stops. She made potatoes, eggs, country bacon, sausage, and French toast. Normally she would make just sausage and eggs mixed, or some potatoes, eggs, and maybe some fatback, but never the breakfast she made that morning. I was grateful for it, though, and hell, it was delicious. While I was eating my food, my phone rang. I got up to grab it, and it was Tanya.

"Hello," I answered.

"Hey, Miss Thang," she sang into the phone.

She liked calling me "Miss thang" for whatever reason.

I said, "Hey, I called you last night, but the line was busy."

Dryly she said, "Oh, I had company last night. Maybe someone was using the phone. So, Miss Thang, I called to find out what time you'll be headed this way? I have a few things I need to do today?"

I said, "I'm eating breakfast right now and will head that way as soon as I'm done. Give me about an hour."

She said, "Can you stop and get a money order for your half of the rent?"

Confused, I said, "Huh? I just paid you rent two weeks ago."

She said, "Yeah, but it's the 1st of the month, and rent is due again. Just look at it as paying your first and last month. Besides, I had to pay twice when I moved in, but that's just how it goes."

"Okay," I said.

I should have known then that something wasn't right. I don't know what I was thinking. I just knew that I was ready to get out of my grandparent's house.

I finished up breakfast, and my granddaddy helped me

move my things. It only took a little over an hour to move in and set up my bed. I ended up paying rent again that day which took a huge chunk out of what I was saving, but I wanted to be grown and responsible, so I guess that went with the territory.

CHAPTER 17

THE TRUTH ABOUT A LIE

When I moved in, Tanya told me that she was going to add me to the lease when she took the money orders to the rental office. I was happy to know that everything was going to be official. My phone service wouldn't be transferred over until the following day, but I was ok with that.

I started settling in and finally unpacking. I cleaned the closet out so I could hang some of my clothes. It was mostly cleaned out already, but it had some papers on the floor and what looked like empty shopping bags on the shelf.

Tanya yelled from the other room, "I'll be back, Miss Thang!"

"Okay!" I yelled back.

I pulled down the bags and started picking up the paper from the floor. Turns out the papers were shopping receipts. I looked at them and noticed they were for random accessories, but mostly handbags. It struck me as odd because Tanya's old roommate's name was Regina or Gigi for short, but the receipts had different people's names on them. I thought maybe these were Gigi's relatives or friends.

Either way, I threw it all in the trash. Hell, if she wanted it, she wouldn't have left it behind.

I finished unpacking my things, and I was impressed with how my room looked. Tanya hadn't returned yet, so I decided to use her phone to call Manny. The phone rang about four or five times, and just when I was about to hang up, someone answered.

"Speak!" the voice boomed into the phone.

"Um, uh, Manny?" I said.

The voice chuckled, "Nah, this ain't him." Then muffled, I could hear the voice say, "Manny, come get the phone."

"Who is it?" I heard Manny ask.

In the background, it sounded like they were having a party.

The voice asked, "May I ask who's calling?"

I said, "This is Blu, but I can call him back if he's busy."

The voice said, "Blu! How are you doing?"

I asked, "Who is this?"

The voice said, "This is Dawg!"

I said, "Oh! Hey, how are you?"

Dawg said, "I'm good. I heard you got your own spot now, congrats!"

I replied, "Thanks."

Just as Dawg was about to say something else, I could hear the phone wrestling around a little bit, then Manny's voice chimed in.

He said, "Hey baby, are you all moved in?"

"Damn nigga," Dawg said in the background.

I said, "Yeah, I just finished up."

Manny said, "Did you change your number?"

Confused, I said, "Huh?"

At first, I didn't understand the question, but then I

realized he might have been referring to the number that appeared on the caller ID.

"No," I said, and then continued, "I'm just using my cousin's phone because my service will not be transferred until tomorrow."

"Oh, ok," he said.

Curious, I asked, "What's going on over there? Sounds like you guys are having a party or something?"

He said, "Nah, it's not like that. I just have a few friends over, Dawg, Psycho, and two other cats from the neighborhood."

The background noise started to get louder. It almost sounded like a commotion was taking place.

So, I said, "Oh, well, we will talk later. Go ahead and tend to your company. I don't want you to be rude."

"Okay, baby, I'll call you later," he said and then hung up before I could even say goodbye.

I wasn't mad, though. Manny always acted like that when his friends were around. Sometimes Dawg would end up taking over the conversation as if he enjoyed talking to me. I think Dawg liked me, and Manny knew it because he would always rush Dawg off the phone whenever he would get too chatty. It was always an innocent conversation, but Manny didn't care for his friends talking to me, period. It didn't matter to him what we were talking about.

I'm not sure what time Tanya came back in the house. After I got off the phone with Manny, I curled up to a good book. I must've fallen asleep reading because I was startled awake by the fire alarm going off. I jumped up and ran to the kitchen to see what the hell was going on. Tanya was in there cooking, and it was super smoky even though I didn't smell anything burning.

"What's with all the smoke?" I asked.

"I think something spilled in the oven. That damn smoke detector goes off every time I use it," she replied.

"Maybe it just needs to be cleaned," I said.

Tanya didn't say anything. She just cut her eyes over at me. I don't know what I said wrong. I was just trying to help her out. It was awkwardly silent, so I offered her a hand.

"Do you need help with anything?" I asked.

She said, "No, dinner will be ready in a few minutes, Miss Thang."

"Oh, okay," I said and took a seat at the table.

I sparked up a random conversation with her about work. I told her about what it was like working for The Uniform Store, and she started telling me about all the juicy gossip from where she worked. She told me how she and Gigi worked together at the credit card company.

Tanya said, "Gigi is making bank up there, and everyone in the processing department be eating out the palm of her hands."

Gigi was a redbone with good hair. In my opinion, she thought she was the shit.

"Why did Gigi move out if things were good between y'all?" I asked.

"She moved in with her rich African boyfriend who wanted to take care of her. I can't say that I blame her either! While he pays the bills, she can bank all her money," Tanya explained.

Tanya pulled the food from the oven and sat it on the counter.

She announced, "Dinner is done. You can fix your plate."

I got up and went over to fix my plate and then sat back down to eat. She had made some kind of chicken and rice dish. I think it was supposed to be jerk chicken, but it was kind of bland, and the rice was not done all the way. I just ate it quietly because I didn't want to hurt her feelings and tell her that her food wasn't good. After dinner, I cleaned up the kitchen and went to take my shower so that I could get ready for bed.

The weekend went by fast. Tanya and I ended up going out to a club on Sunday night. I didn't want to go at first because I had to work the next day, but I decided to go and enjoy myself. After all, I could sleep in late since I didn't have to be at work until 3 p.m. the next day. Gigi and a few of her friends met us there. It was a gay club, but I had a good time dancing and mingling with some of the people.

Everyone was super friendly and really knew how to have a good time. We chilled at the club until about midnight and ended up stopping by the carryout for some takeout. I was in the mood for some chicken, and the carryout was the only thing still open on a Sunday night. So, I settled for wings and french fries.

Even though we left the club early, I didn't get back home and settled in until after 3 a.m. I was so tired I really didn't feel like taking a shower before bed, but I forced myself. It seemed like I had just fallen asleep when I was startled awake by a knock on my bedroom door.

"Come in," I said.

I knew it was Tanya because we lived alone.

A male voice said, "Excuse me, Miss Blu. Can I use your phone?"

I whipped my neck towards the door so fast I almost caught whiplash. I couldn't seem to form a damn sentence, and I thought I was dreaming. I blinked a few times so my eyes could focus, and sure as shit, a fucking stranger was at my damn bedroom door.

"Who the fuck is this?" I thought to myself.

He said, "I'm sorry to wake you. Your cousin told me to ask if I could use your phone."

Agitated, I said, "Why can't you use her phone?"

"Uh," was all he said before he left from the doorway.

The asshole didn't have the damn decency to even close my door. A few seconds later, I could see Tanya leaving her room and heading my way. She stood in the doorway, seemingly confused as to why I had an attitude.

"What time is it?" I asked before she could even get any words out.

"It's seven o'clock," she said as if that was late or something. She continued, "Miss Thang, I need to use your phone."

I said, "What's wrong with yours, Tanya?"

She replied, "They must've cut it off this morning."

"But why?" I asked.

"I'm late paying the bill, but I will pay it when I can," she said as she grabbed my phone and left out of the room.

I don't even recall telling her that it was ok for her to use it, but whatever. That should've been a red flag for me, and I think it was, but I was tired, so I just ignored it.

I quickly pulled the covers up and turned over to go back to sleep. I would ask her who that guy was later. I dozed back off for a short time but got back up because I had to pee. On the way out of the bathroom, I saw that my phone was still in Tanya's room. I knocked, and there was no answer, so I knocked harder. Still no answer. I opened the door, and just like that, she was gone.

I went into the living room to check the time, and it

was already 12:36 p.m. Damn! I didn't realize it was that late. Tanya must have gone to work since she works from 9 a.m. – 5 p.m. I called my granddaddy to ask him if he could give me a ride to The Uniform Store, and he agreed to come get me. So, I quickly jumped in the shower to freshen up.

On my way out of the bathroom, I heard someone come in through the front door. I froze for a split second because I had no clue who would be coming in. I relaxed when I heard Tanya giggling. I peeked around the corner to get a look at what she was doing and saw her walking in with that same mystery man from earlier that morning. I quickly ducked back around the corner and went into my room so that I could get dressed.

As I was getting dressed, I couldn't help but think about the internal alarms that were going off in my head. Who is this damn dude that has been hanging around since this morning? When did he come over? Why wasn't she able to pay her damn phone bill when I paid rent twice within two weeks? Why isn't her ass at work? I had so many questions, but I knew that this was not the best time to ask.

After getting dressed, I went to the kitchen to put something in my stomach before work. Tanya and the mystery man were sitting at the table eating while making googly eyes at each other.

"Hey," I said.

Tanya looked at me and said, "Miss Thang, this is my friend, Ronnie."

"Randy," he corrected.

"That's what I said," she continued as she cut her eyes over at me as if her ass wasn't busted.

I didn't say a word. I just turned around to make myself a cold-cut sandwich.

"Well, it was nice meeting you, Miss Thang," Randy said.

I said, "Please, call me Blu."

Neither of them responded, and I didn't bother to turn around to look at the expression on either of their faces. I just continued to make my sandwich. When I was done, I left the kitchen to eat it in my room. I didn't want to intrude on whatever it was they called themselves doing out there.

My brain was still trying to process how it was that he was in our crib so early in the damn morning, and she didn't even know his name. Something deep in my soul just didn't feel right. I was finishing up with my sandwich when the phone rang.

"Hello," I answered.

"Hey, baby. What's up?" Manny said.

I said, "Nothing much. Just finished eating, so I can leave out for work in the next few minutes."

Manny said, "I know, that's why I called to tell you to have a good day. I figured you would be leaving soon."

"Thanks," I replied.

I heard the front door close, and I wanted to be nosy to see who was coming in now.

Hurriedly I said, "I'll call you tonight when I get back home."

"Okay, later," Manny said.

I grabbed my bag, walked into the living room, and noticed that the mystery man was gone. Tanya, however, was sitting on the couch looking at the TV.

The first thing that flew out my mouth was, "Where did you meet him?"

"I don't remember," Tanya said with annoyance.

"Clearly. You don't have to work today?" I asked.

She snapped, "What's with all of the questions, Blu?"

"I'm sorry, I was just asking. No need to get your panties in a bunch," I said.

Continuing with her attitude, she said, "If you must know, I called out because I didn't feel like going."

I glanced out of the window and saw that my granddaddy was pulling into the parking lot.

I said, "Okay, well, I will see you later."

On the way out of the building, I noticed that Tanya's new friend was just standing outside leaning on the wall near the entrance of the building.

He said with a mischievous grin, "You have a good day, Miss Blu."

I looked at him suspiciously and said, "You too."

I jumped in the car with my granddaddy and said, "Hey, Granddaddy."

He said, "Hey sweetheart, how was your weekend?"

"It was good," I replied.

We rode in silence most of the way. I wanted to tell my granddaddy about some of the things that had happened, but I didn't want to hear what he had to say. Then I thought about giving Tanya's sister, Kia, a call and talk to her, but I decided against that as well. I guess my granddaddy could sense that something was heavy on my mind.

He said, "Blu is everything alright?"

I said, "Yeah, Granddaddy. Why do you ask?"

He chuckled, "Because you have never been this quiet before."

I replied with the partial truth and said, "Oh, just thinking about some bills and what I'll have to pay as soon as I get my check on Friday."

He said, "Well, if you ever want to talk, you know you can call me."

I looked at him with a smile and said, "I know."

My granddaddy dropped me off at work, and I went in to start my shift.

After that day, everything was going great, at least for two months. Tanya and I had a routine going. We both worked, paid our portion of the bills, and bought food for the house. But I did most of the cooking because she couldn't cook very well. In exchange, Tanya would help clean the kitchen when I prepared the meal. She tried to cook a few times; it was just never enjoyable. I think the only time she stepped in to cook was on those occasional days she didn't feel like cleaning the kitchen.

She never did get her phone service turned back on. I'm not sure if it was because she was comfortable with using mine, or she just didn't want to kick out the money for another bill. We went half on all the bills except my phone bill. We should've gone half on that bill too. She used it as much as I did, but I didn't complain since I had the money to pay it.

We went out to party at least three or four times a week, which was easy since Kia and her ex-boo Daniel owned the Safari Club. Daniel was cool, and I could tell he was fond of me, but he didn't care for Tanya that much. He thought she was a messy hoe.

He said, "Every time she come around, people end up mad at each other and arguing over what someone supposedly said or didn't say."

I must admit, he wasn't wrong because there was always drama and commotion whenever a group of people got around her. Daniel didn't like all that fighting and bickering in his establishment. So, we hung out at other clubs as well, but it seemed like we always ended our night at the

Safari Club. What can I say? It was owned by family, and we got in free.

Gigi hung out with us a few times, but we didn't see much of her because she would go out of town every week. She'd come back from New York with all kinds of designer bags, shoes, scarfs, belts, and other accessories. Gigi was living the good life, or so I thought. I was trying to figure out how I could convince a rich African to take care of me too.

After a while, it seemed like we were going out almost every night. I was a trooper, though, because no matter how many times I hung out, I still took my ass to work. Tanya, not so much. It seemed like she was calling out from work more and more. As a matter of fact, her calling out became part of the routine. I didn't care, though. As long as she was paying her part of the bills, what could I say?

One night while we were hanging out at the Safari, Kia approached us.

She said, "Y'all can make some money up in here!"

"How?" Tanya said excitedly.

Kia boasted, "All we need to do is set up some type of concession stand. I mean, look at this place. We could be booming!"

Tanya rolled her eyes and said, "Nope, I'm not interested."

Personally, I didn't think it would be a bad idea. I mean, we could sell chili dogs, chips, and drinks. Hell, we could get fancy and sell pizza by the slice. Kia definitely had a great idea. As I looked around, I zoned out, thinking about the money we could make. I figured I'd bring it up to her another time once I sat down and put some digits behind the thought. It's easy to say no to something when you aren't thinking about the potential it has.

The next day I was cleaning and daydreaming when my phone rang.

I answered, "Hello."

The male caller said, "Tanya, please."

I said, "She's at work."

The male caller questioned, "You sure? I just talked to her, and she told me she didn't have to work today."

Irritated, I said, "Well, she's not here. I can take a message and have her call you back."

"Just tell her Psycho called," he said and then hung up.

I looked at the phone, confused. The only Psycho I knew was Manny's friend Psycho. Why the hell would he be calling Tanya? How does he even know her? I hung up and then pressed *69 on the phone to capture the number. I wrote down the number the operator gave. I didn't know what was going on, but I was going to get down to the bottom of it.

I thought about what he said, "She wasn't at work."

Hmph! It must be nice. I finished cleaning up and then got ready for work.

CHAPTER 18

CARELESS WHISPERING

On my way home from work, my mind was still puzzled by the call from Psycho. When I came in the apartment, I was shocked to see Tanya entertaining company. It was Tanya, Gigi, and Retta, who was a friend of Gigi, sitting on the couch. Things felt weird, and they were unusually quiet. Normally they were extra chatty.

I said, "Hey y'all, what's up?"

"Hey," they said in unison.

You could hear a pin drop in that room. I was under the impression my presence wasn't welcomed, so I decided to go to my room and call Manny before it got too late.

When I called, I didn't get an answer which was strange because normally he'd wait up for my call. I didn't sweat the issue because I'd figured he probably fell asleep. So, I got up to go take a shower. As I approached my door, I could hear Gigi whispering. I knew I shouldn't have been eavesdropping, but I wanted to know what was going on.

I slightly opened my door just enough to hear a little

better. I still couldn't make out everything that was being said, but I could hear bits and pieces.

Gigi said, "I didn't say your name."

"So why do they want to meet with me?" Tanya asked.

Gigi said, "Probably because they know we're close and used to live together."

I didn't understand what they were talking about. So, I purposely left out of my room and headed to the kitchen to get a drink. Honestly, I wanted to catch more of what they were talking about.

As soon as I rounded the corner, Tanya cleared her throat, and just like that, they were all quiet again. What were these bitches up to? I grabbed a bottle of water out of the fridge and headed back to my room.

I stopped and said, "Hey, are we going out tonight?"

"Nah." She replied flatly.

I don't know why that pissed me off, but it did. When I got to my room, I left my door cracked and sat on my bed. Immediately the whispering started again. I decided to just brush it off.

As my grandmother always said, "Everything done in the dark comes to light."

Minding my business, I got up and went to take my shower. When I got out of the shower, they were still in there whispering. I didn't care. I closed my door completely and went to bed.

The next morning when I woke up, my phone had been removed from my room again. I didn't mind Tanya using my phone, but the least she could do was return it. I went into Tanya's room to get my phone, and when I opened the door, I was in for a rude awakening. Tanya was in there, knocked out with some dude that was completely naked. He wasn't bad-looking; he just looked ashy. I couldn't help but glance down at his dick that was dried up and stuck to his leg.

I thought, "Nasty mutha fuckers."

It was obvious that they had been fucking and didn't bother washing off afterward. I grabbed my phone and went to my room. She was just in the living room last night talking with Gigi and Retta. When the hell did this dude come over, and who the fuck was he? We didn't go anywhere last night, so why'd she call in again?

I tried to call Manny when I got back to my room, and again I got no answer. I didn't think too much about it. It was payday, and I was in a good mood. So, I went into the living room, turned on some music, and started cleaning up. About twenty minutes later, Tanya came into the living room looking worn out.

"Are you ok?" I asked.

"Yeah, just tired," she responded as she took a seat on the couch.

"Who's that in your room?" I asked.

She glanced up at me with a puzzled look and said, "How do you know I have someone in my room?"

I said, "I'm sorry, I thought you were at work and went in your room to get my phone."

She replied, "He's a friend of mine."

Nonchalantly I said, "Ok. It's Friday! Are we going out tonight?"

"Maybe," she said.

"We haven't been out in two days. That's unlike us," I said.

"Look, Miss Thang, I'm just gonna be straight with you," she said.

At this point, she had my full attention.

She went on, "Gigi got fired from the credit card

company, and because we're friends, I'm now under investigation too for this little credit card scam that was going on. But the details aren't important. What you need to know is that I've been suspended while they do the investigation."

Thinking back to the bits and pieces of their conversation, it was all making sense now. Gigi was stealing credit cards and taking them out of town to get merchandise which explained the receipts I found when I first moved in a little over three months ago. Damn, how long had this been going on? Tanya had been suspended for a whole week, but Gigi was terminated that same day.

I said, "So, when do you find out when you can go back to work?"

She said, "I have a meeting with them on Monday."

Trying to encourage her, I said, "I wouldn't worry about it too much! They would have fired you already if they had something on you."

She rolled her eyes as if I said something wrong and then went back into her room. I didn't know what her problem was, but her attitude stunk. She would often roll her eyes, keep secrets, do shiesty shit and act as if we weren't cool for some reason.

A few moments later, Tanya and her company emerged from her room. Her company was fully dressed and visibly agitated as he left the apartment.

Tanya turned to me and said, "Miss Thang, we're going out tonight! I thought about what you said, and you're right. I wasn't in the mood to go at first, but I changed my mind."

She came over and helped me clean the rest of the kitchen, and we sat around talking for a few hours until it was time for me to get ready for work.

Things went back to normal for the next three weeks or so. Tanya was cleared of any wrongdoing at the processing center. Although they suspected her in the credit card scam, they couldn't find any evidence of her involvement. Therefore, she was able to return to work. As for her attitude switch up, I chalked it up to simply me being paranoid. Now we were back to working, paying bills, and hanging out at different clubs most of the week.

One Saturday morning, I heard a loud knock at the door. So, I got up to see who it was. I looked at the clock on the wall in the living room, and it was already after 11 a.m. I glanced back, and Tanya's door was still closed. We'd just gotten in from the club a few hours prior. I looked through the peephole and then opened the door for a distressed Gigi. Before I could even open the damn door all the way, she had pushed her way inside.

Concerned, I asked, "What's wrong?"

Hysterical, she blurted out, "Where's Tanya?"

She headed in the direction of Tanya's room, and before she could reach for the door, a man opened Tanya's door and walked out of her room.

I didn't have to look hard to figure out that I had never seen him before. What was up with her and all these random men? Gigi walked past the guy and straight to Tanya's bedside.

She screamed, "HE FUCKING PUT ME OUT!"

Tanya jumped up, gently pushed her company in the hallway, and closed her bedroom door. He just stood there looking stupid. Then he looked at me and shrugged his shoulders as if I had asked him a question.

I wasn't about to miss out on all Gigi's drama, so I sat on the end of the couch with my hand resting under my chin. I guess Mr. Strange-nigga got tired of just standing there, so he sat on the other end of the sofa.

He whispered, "Can I ask you a question?"

I said, "You just did."

He chuckled and then said, "What do you want?"

I said, "Huh? I don't understand the question. What do you mean, what do I want? This is my place, ain't it?"

He scooted closer to me on the couch and leaned in close. He was just about to say something when we heard a noise from the hallway. He quickly scooted back to his end of the couch as if he was not supposed to talk to me. Tanya's door opened, and Gigi made a beeline for the bathroom. I assumed she wanted to straighten her face, but it was too late because I already saw that she had been crying.

Tanya looked at me with wide eyes before giving Mr. Strange a smirk. She then motioned for him to return to the room. Tanya whispered something to him and then came and sat next to me on the couch. Mr. Strange went back in her room and then closed the door.

I said, "What the fuck was that all about?"

She said, "Miss Thang, the shit done hit the fan, but I will fill you in as soon as she leaves."

I said, "Okay," and then went into my room.

Later Tanya came into my room to let me in on what happened. She explained how Gigi's man had been having an affair with some white chick. Gigi had caught him on several occasions. She'd get mad at him and threaten to leave, but he wouldn't leave the white girl alone. So, Gigi decided to just drop the issue instead and allow him to do whatever he wanted since he was taking care of her. That plan was fine and dandy until he decided to fully replace her with the white girl. He kicked Gigi's ass to the curb like a bad habit. When Tanya finished telling me everything, all I could do was shake my head.

"Where will she go?" I asked.

She said, "You let her worry about that, Miss Thang unless you're going to offer up your room?"

And with that said, Tanya went back to her room to finish entertaining Mr. Strange.

I sat on my bed in thought for a moment. Life is funny sometimes. Less than a year ago, Gigi was on top of the world just for all of it to be taken away from her a short while later.

The next day, Tanya and I went clubbing, as usual and hung out until about one in the morning. We had such a great time at the club that we didn't wind ourselves down and head to bed until almost 4 a.m. And as usual, 9 a.m. came around too quickly for Tanya, and she decided to call in.

Her boss said, "No problem, but don't bother coming back tomorrow either because you're fired."

I guess Tanya called in one too many times for them, but I think they had it in for her ever since that credit card scam case. While they didn't have evidence to fire her for the credit card scam, they were able to use her poor attendance to get rid of her once and for all.

After Tanya got fired, she quickly realized that she had to do something so that she could pay her portion of the bills. Even though I always had my half, I helped her work side jobs so that she could have her half also. So, we decided to do food service at The Safari Club, as Kia had suggested.

When Kia first suggested it, Tanya didn't want to do it. Now she had no choice because the bills would not pay themselves. It turned out to be a great idea because we were booming right out the gate. We made money hand over fist and sold out of many of our items.

Daniel approached me one day and said, "What do you think about helping me with the front door? You'd frisk the females and collect money."

Daniel didn't trust Tanya with the money, so he was fine with her staying in the back working the foodservice. Tanya felt some kind of way about that, but she never voiced it to me.

Daniel and I walked to the front of the club so he could show me exactly what he wanted me to do. Up at the front, Kia was talking to the male bouncer who was in charge of frisking the males as they entered the club. The bouncer had just finished checking Randy, who I remembered seeing at the apartment with Tanya.

"Hi Randy," I said.

"Hey," he replied as he continued through the entryway.

"You know him?" Kia asked me.

I replied, "Not like that, but he spent the night with your sister some time ago."

Kia didn't respond, but I saw the look of disgust on her face.

I asked, "What's wrong?"

Kia pulled me to the side.

She said, "I keep trying to tell Tanya to leave these no-good niggas alone. They're just using her. She keeps hooking up with all these different guys but sleeping with them is not going to keep them around."

Tanya, however, was hardheaded. She would do the opposite of what her sister told her to do.

Daniel walked over and said, "Ok, Blu, follow me. I

want to show you a few more things before you get started tonight."

From that night on, I learned as much as I could and began working in the front. It wasn't long before Tanya became noticeably jealous.

She often said, "You need to be helping me in the back with food service."

But I was doing them both. I'd help Tanya when it was too busy for her to do alone, and I would also help at the front. We were bringing in a lot of money and doing good, despite the fact Tanya's attitude toward me was changing, or at least that's how I felt.

A couple of weeks had passed, and strangely I still hadn't heard from Manny. I'd come in from working the club, got settled for bed, then I tried to hit Manny's line again. I knew that he was ok because people had seen him around the way. It was really starting to bother me that he was being so distant. I wondered if he was purposely avoiding me and why? I decided to blind call him, so I dialed *67 and then called. This time he answered after the third ring.

He answered in a deep tone, trying to disguise his voice. "Hello?"

With attitude, I said, "Oh, so it's true! You are avoiding me!"

In his normal voice, he replied, "I'm not avoiding you. I just needed some time."

I said, "I'm about to give you all the time you need. Just answer one question for me. Are you talking to my cousin behind my back?"

"Is that what you think?" he asked.

"It has been weeks, and it seems to me like you're both switching up on me. You're missing in action, not answering my calls, and she's acting all wishy-washy toward me. Nothing else makes sense!"

Silence.

I yelled, "Say something!"

He said, "Why do you think I'm talking to her behind your back?"

I said, "For starters, a while back, Psycho called her. I copied the number and started looking through the caller I.D. Guess what I found? That wasn't the first, nor the last, time the number showed up in the call history. Are you getting Psycho to call here so that you can talk to her?"

Silence.

"You know what, I guess I have my answer. Goodbye, Manny."

"Wait," he finally blurted out.

"I'm listening," I said with attitude.

"I have something to tell you, but please don't be mad at me."

Rolling my eyes as if he could see me, I replied, "I said I'm listening."

He said, "The truth is I knew you before A.J. introduced us."

I'd always thought it was strange that we lived so close to each other but never met. I was intrigued. How did I not remember meeting him before?

He continued, "I saw you for the first time at my man T-Rex's house."

I cycled through my mental rolodex and said, "T-Rex? Are you sure you aren't mistaking me for someone else?"

He chuckled, "I'm sure it was you. I saw you several times before then, but that was the first time we spoke."

I said, "But I don't know anyone named T-Rex."

Manny said, "Yeah, you came in with his sister Tiffany."

Then it clicked, and I said, "Wait! Are you talking about Tiffany's brother Twon?"

"Yes, we call him T-Rex," he said.

I realized he was talking about the day Justice and I cut class after the incident in the cafeteria, and we all went back to Tiffany's house. I still didn't remember seeing him there, though.

I said, "It's a small world. But wait, you were there that day?"

He replied, "Yeah. Psycho and Dawg were there too. I don't blame you for cutting out the way you did that day."

"Why you say that?" I asked.

Manny went on to tell me that Psycho raped Tiffany that day and how he thought Tanya was the one that set it up. I couldn't believe what he was saying, but I didn't take him for being the type to lie, over exaggerate, or make things up either. I kept trying to rewind that day back in my mind, but from what I remembered, Tiffany looked like she was enjoying herself.

I questioned, "Why do you think it was rape, and why do you think Tanya had something to do with it?"

He said, "Because of the way it happened. When you and Justice left, Tanya and Psycho were in the back room. I don't know what they were in there doing, but twenty minutes later, Tanya came out and told Tiffany that Psycho wanted her."

Fully engaged, I said, "Okay, and then what happened?"

He went on, "Tiffany ignored her, but Tanya was persistent. She was like, Tiffany. I know you heard me. Tiffany was like, no, tell him to come out here."

"That's odd," I said.

Manny said, "Tanya kept at it, telling Tiffany that he had something to show her until finally, Tiffany went in the room with him. A few minutes later, all you heard was a bunch of thumping, screaming, and what sounded like glass breaking, like they were fighting. A few minutes more went by, then Psycho came out with fresh scratches on his face fixing his pants. He barked, LET'S G.O., and we left."

I sat on the edge of my bed, digesting all that Manny had just said. I instantly felt bad for Tiffany. I remember her parents pulling her out of that school and putting her into private school. I thought it was because of what happened in the cafeteria that day, but now I see it was something way worse. I'd heard stories about Tiffany being a freak and how she would allow guys to feel her up, but that didn't make what he did to her right. Psycho straight up violated her.

Angry, I said, "So y'all just left? Where was Twon? What did he do?"

"Yes, I left! And what could Twon do?" Manny shouted.

"What do you mean? Report it to the police, beat Psycho's ass—I don't know, but something." I said.

He explained, "Listen, Blu, that nigga carries a gun. When he starts waving his gun around, if you don't do what he says, he will shoot your ass, plain and simple. It doesn't matter who you are. There was nothing Twon could do, and me, Dawg, Tanya, and Psycho all rolled out. Dawg and I were in the back seat scared to death, while Tanya and Psycho sat upfront laughing and passing a joint back and forth like nothing ever happened."

In anger, I said, "I can't stand Psycho's ass, and I'll be glad when he gets what's coming to him."

I wondered why Tanya never mentioned this to me. I mean, at least say something about Tiffany being raped, but

I guess saying anything would've associated her with it, and that's not something she wanted, especially if she set that girl up.

I added, "That nigga is bad news, and you need to stop hanging around him before he gets you into some trouble you can't get out of."

Skipping over my comment, he said, "Imagine my shock when I found out that Tanya was your cousin!"

I'd never told Manny that Tanya was my cousin because I didn't want to mess things up with him. I didn't want to be judged based on Tanya's reputation. I wanted to keep all negativity out of our friendship.

Manny continued, "And for the record, it's not like I hang around him because I want to. Sometimes I don't have a choice, especially when they all show up at my house unannounced and say come take a ride with us."

I said, "Yeah, that's kinda messed up."

"Honestly, I'm surprised A.J. gave me your number. It was Dawg that kept asking him about you."

Surprised, I said, "Wait, what?"

"Dawg asked A.J. about you several times. He even asked about you when we saw you at T-Rex's house. Everybody else was trying to holla at Justice, but Dawg and I liked you. My mistake was telling Dawg that I liked you when I first saw you around the way," he said.

"Why a mistake?" I asked.

"Because he always tries to either outdo me or beat me to the punch. If I see a fresh pair of kicks I like and want to get, he'll go cop them first. If I say I like a girl, he starts pushing up on her. I said I liked you. Next thing I know, he was pressing A.J. to hook y'all up. But A.J. gave M.E. your number, even though I never asked, and told Dawg to stay away from you or else he'd break his neck."

I was blown away by all the things Manny told me. We went from radio silence to literally hours of chatting. He told me about how A.J. once viciously beat Psycho up at a playground and how to this day, A.J. is the one person Psycho fears. Then he told me how Psycho became a psycho. I'm not going to lie, though. It was sad to hear about how Psycho was physically and sexually abused and even pimped out to men by his aunt as a child. This went on for years. She kept him quiet by threatening to kill him and his mom and said that if it got out, his family in Nigeria would disown him.

I continued to listen to Manny go on about Psycho and his childhood issues. Apparently, that's why he felt women were nasty and needed to be treated like whores. While I felt what happened to him was awful, I still didn't agree with him violating others. I don't care what anyone said.

Manny asked, "Do you know light-skinned Ingrid that lives two buildings over from you?"

I said, "Yeah, I know Ingrid. She's the girl that fell off the balcony, right?"

"Yeah, that's the one! Well, that wasn't an accident."

I said, "What you mean it wasn't an accident?"

He said, "Psycho raped her and threw her off the balcony. Then he told her that if she told anyone, he would come back and kill her."

I screamed, "What? Why are you telling me all this?"

It felt like our conversation had become a confessional for Manny. I was drawn and glued to the information, but it was too much to bear.

I said, "We need to be telling these stories to the police. He really needs to be picked up off the street Manny."

He said, "I know, but he's crazy! That's why a lot of times, when they come over, I tell my mom to say I'm not here. I don't want to be a part of what they got going on. I fear one day they're going to do something that I'll take the fall for."

I said, "You keep saying them."

Manny said, "I'm talking about Psycho and Dawg. They're together most of the time. I'm not sure if he was there when Psycho threw Ingrid off the balcony, but I've heard stories about them raping girls together."

I interjected, "Ok, I've heard enough. This is just too much. This is making me so uncomfortable."

Manny said, "You know what, you're right. Let's just get off the subject altogether. So, tell me a bedtime story Blu."

I chuckled, "A bedtime story? About what?"

In his sexy voice, he said, "A fantasy about us meeting for the first time. Pretend you were the girl that lived next door."

I just laughed. We both enjoyed telling stories, and for the rest of that night, we took turns making up stories about us being together. That was the extent of us going together—we talked on the phone, went for walks while holding hands, and from time to time would kiss. We wouldn't get down and dirty with it, just a peck on the lips. What we had with each other was beautiful. It was literally puppy love—sweet, precious, and innocent puppy love.

CHAPTER 19

TRICKIN' AIN'T EASY

Tanya continued to entertain random men for weeks on end. However, she did manage to throw in a few repeats here and there. The problem was she began spending some of the rent money to buy extra groceries to cook for some of them. She used to go all out for this one guy named Buddy. She'd buy expensive cuts of meat from the store, then come home and ask me to cook it. Of course, she'd front like she cooked it, trying to impress him. Her goal was to snag him in the hopes that he would start paying all her bills. In the end, the joke was on her. All she got in return was a sore mouth and a horrible rash on her coochie.

That was Tanya for you, though. She was always trying to be the hostess with the mostess. She entertained all types of dudes. One night she called herself trying to reel in a big fish and brought home this guy named David. He was one of the big-time dealers in the city. When she came home that evening, David was in tow with a bag of groceries. She claimed David paid for the food, but I knew she had bought the food by the look on David's face.

He looked up, surprised, and chuckled when he heard his name.

The look on his face said, "Girl, you need to stop lying to your little cousin like that. You know I didn't pay for no damn food."

Yes, I heard all of that in his chuckle and facial expression. I could not stand David, though. He made me sick to my stomach with his arrogance and the "women of the world worship me" attitude. He thought he was God's gift to women. Truth is, he had a face only his mother could love. I, myself, hated looking at him because he had a bad acne problem. I'm talking about the kind of acne that leaves huge craters in your face. But no matter what he looked like or how much of an asshole he was, Tanya wanted him and had an ulterior motive.

In true Tanya fashion, she invited more people over to the house, so I headed for the kitchen to begin cooking. Gigi came and bought her boyfriend Spencer, who just so happened to be David's main man. Unlike David, Spencer was easy on the eyes, and I'm not just saying that because standing next to David, everybody was. I'm saying it because he really was handsome. Spencer was easy-going and kind-hearted, but he was also David's hitter. He would be the one that would put in that work whenever David needed something done if you know what I mean.

Kia had given us the lowdown on David and Spencer at the club a long time ago. She told us to stay away from them because they were very dangerous and certainly not the type of men that any of us should be dealing with. But Tanya didn't listen. Instead, Tanya introduced Spencer to Gigi so that Gigi could try to gank Spencer's money while she tried to gank David for his.

I put the food on and immediately went into my room to call Kia and let her know who was at the house.

I said, "The chicken will be done in forty-five minutes."

Kia replied, "And I'll be there in forty. So, set an extra plate."

"You got it, baby," I said.

I got off the phone feeling a little better about creature feature and his friend, knowing Kia would be on her way soon. I knew Tanya would get upset when she saw Kia because she knew David had the hots for Kia.

Tanya and her company were all chilling in the living room, drinking wine, laughing, and giggling, when suddenly there was a knock at the door. I quickly jumped up from the table to get it since I knew exactly who it was.

I yelled, "I'll get it!"

As I opened the door, I said, "Hey Kia! What are you doing here?"

Walking in like she was invited, Kia said, "I was in the neighborhood handling some business and stopped by to check on you and make sure you were alright."

"I'm glad you're here. I'm in here trying to cook that recipe you gave me for roasted herb chicken," I said.

In all my haste to go call Kia earlier, I didn't realize that I had set the wrong temperature for the chicken to completely cook. So, when I took the chicken out of the oven, it wasn't done. David came in the kitchen and saw the pale chicken.

He chuckled and yelled, "Put that chicken back in the oven, baby. It needs a little more color."

I thought to myself, "Oh, now you want to come in the kitchen to help, too late to play sous-chef now."

He was just showing off for Kia.

He turned to her and said, "Can I pour you a glass of wine?"

The nerve of him. I didn't know that guests were supposed to offer people drinks at other people's houses, but I didn't say a word.

Kia laughed at his gesture and said, "Sure, David. That would be just lovely."

Spencer chimed in, "Why don't I go get some liquor, and we can make it a real party."

David said, "Good idea. I'll ride with you."

Spencer grabbed his keys from the coffee table, and they left for the store. As soon as the door closed good, Tanya turned to Kia.

Agitated, Tanya said, "What are you doing over here for real?"

Kia said, "Like I told you, I was handling business in the neighborhood and decided to stop by for a bit."

"So, you're telling me that you ain't have nothing going on tonight at the club?"

"Nope, not a damn thing. I came over here to hang and kick it with y'all for a few, and I see I came right on time for the festivities," Kia said as she sipped on her glass of wine.

Kia turned and looked at Gigi's expression, then busted out laughing. I looked to see what Kia was laughing at and couldn't help but laugh myself. Gigi had on her resting bitch face. It was clear to Gigi that the night wouldn't go how she thought it would, and for that, she was over all of it. Tanya, pissed, just sucked her teeth and rolled her eyes.

David and Spencer returned with plenty of drinks. I don't know what they were trying to accomplish, but they had enough booze to ensure that every one of us could get drunk twice if we wanted to. For a moment, we were all having a nice time. Even Tanya had made it out of her mood. We were laughing, drinking, listening to music, and just joking around. I'm not exactly sure how, but the conversations started getting sexual, and they were all teasing each other. Not sure who, but someone said something teasing Tanya.

Then, Tanya replied, "Oh yeah? I heard that Blu is the one that can give good head."

I was sitting on the floor Indian style with my back against the kitchen counter.

I looked up and said, "What the hell did you just say, Tanya?"

Laughing, she said, "I said, talk around the club is you give good head."

Clearly offended, I jumped up from the floor.

"That's a lie!" I screamed.

"Calm down, I was only joking with you," she said, laughing even harder.

I sat back down with a straight face while she continued to laugh.

I said, "I don't think that's funny."

David, who was sitting in the chair near me, then pulled his dick out and tried to touch me with it.

Agitated, I jumped up and yelled, "Oh, hell no! Get away from me and leave me alone!"

Kia said, "That's enough, David. You're too full because now you're starting to clown."

David continued flicking his dick at me.

Kia repeated, "David, that's enough! Either put your dick away or get the hell out."

David looked at me and said, "Blu, I'll pay you if you suck me off."

I said, "Are you crazy? Hell no! You must be on that stuff."

"Well, how much would it take?" he said as he pulled a wad of cash from his pocket.

He placed five $100 bills on the table and repeated his ask.

He said, "If you give me head right now, I will give you all five of these crisp one-hundred-dollar bills."

I don't know why he thought that would change my mind. Who did he think I was, Tanya?

I said, "Hell No! Not ever! Screw you, your cat, and your dog!"

Tanya said, "Girl, are you crazy? We need that for rent money!"

I turned to her and said, "No, I don't need it for rent, and if you need the money that bad, then you go suck his little dick."

The room was quiet as everyone else watched the saga unfold.

David laughed and said, "Girl, my dick would knock all of your front teeth out."

It was my turn to laugh, and laugh I did as I replied, "Not mine. You better aim for Tanya's teeth because that ain't the kind of shit I'm into."

Everybody started laughing and joking except Tanya, who was now upset. She actually wanted me to do it and take that man's money. She caught a serious attitude with me and kept telling me how we needed the money.

I finally said, "Then you know what you need to do, Tanya, because I'm not down with that."

Then she said, "Oh okay, I see Miss Thang, you think you're too good. You're just a little goody-two-shoes and Kia's little snitch."

I said, "Whatever," then turned and walked away.

Tanya was pissed with me for the rest of the evening.

David ended up spending the night, and they screwed for half of it. She thought she was in for a nice payday, but she didn't get not one red cent. Her blow job must've been on the house because she didn't even get the $500 that he offered me. I understand she was mad, but she shouldn't hate the player. She should hate the game. Maybe she should go back and read the rules again because obviously, she wasn't playing it right.

Kia always gave us pep talks and instructions on what to do if things got tight.

She would say, "Don't y'all go out and be screwing all of these men because all they want to do is use your body. So, don't give it to them. If you say no, they'll say yes to whatever we want."

Apparently, Tanya wanted to do things her way because, for some reason, she couldn't get that through her sick, nasty, promiscuous, and adulterated skull. She reminded me of my mother, always trying to run game, but instead got game ran on them.

I didn't have anything to do with what she didn't get from that man. I knew she was upset, but I didn't realize just how upset she was until eight days later, when she still wasn't talking to me. I couldn't believe this simple chick had the nerve to still be mad and carry a damn grudge. This couldn't have been about me turning David down. Tanya knew I would never go for anything like that. No, this had to be something else.

Tanya was really jealous and upset with her sister. Honestly, I think she was mad because she knew I called Kia to come over that night. But hell, everybody knew David liked Kia, including her, and she still pursued him. But as usual, she took her anger with Kia out on me.

I guess what they say is true; hindsight is always 20/20.

At first, I thought Tanya actually cared about me. Clearly, I was wrong because it became more evident that she only cared about herself. I noticed how she always conjured up mischief. She'd try to take advantage of her friends and family that loved her but break her neck to submit to those no-good niggas out in the street running game.

She was a prime example of the saying, "What you put out in the atmosphere will come back to you."

At some point after that failed dinner party, Tanya started tricking for money. I guess it was her way of making her half of the rent that she often spent trying to impress these dudes. More and more random men became the trend for her. She would often take me on escapades with her hoping to set me up with the guy's friend. But that wasn't my thang, that's what she and Gigi did.

I knew what she was trying to do, but I went along anyway just for support and security because she would always find herself in crazy situations. Most of the time, they would just get mad at me because I didn't want anybody to touch me. I didn't have sex with anyone, and I didn't drink nothing that anybody gave me. I think me not going along to get along made her resent me. I just didn't want to be out there sexing random dudes knowing I had a boyfriend at home. I wasn't even sexing him, so why would I think about hooking up with a random for a one-night stand?

The guys we went out with often referred to me as "the square" and then would complain to Tanya.

They'd say, "Why you bring your "mother" along?"

In truth, I never wanted to be there. I only went along with her because I cared about her and her safety. I don't know what I would have done if something had happened to her. I thought I was doing the right thing.

A few times, I talked to Kia about it out of concern. Sometimes I'd give her our whereabouts or the 4-1-1 on what we were doing, just so someone knew what was going on. Kia wasn't happy at all, to say the least. I guess she mentioned it to Tanya at some point because Tanya approached me about it.

Furious, she said, "You don't need to tell my sister MY business. I don't want Kia to know anything that I don't tell her myself."

Honestly, I didn't tell all her business. I just told Kia when I didn't feel comfortable or when she would have us around grimy looking dudes--the ones that would rob or harm you. Either way, Tanya just didn't care.

She was so pissed with me she made the comment, "That's ok, I will fix it."

Whatever the fuck that meant. She gave me the cold shoulder and silent treatment briefly, but that eventually faded after a while. Then we slowly got back to how things used to be, or so I thought.

I had a break from the club one night and went home to take a nice shower after my full-time job. I had been going nonstop for seven days straight, so I wanted to enjoy my downtime. After I got out the shower, I applied my favorite lotion and put on my nightclothes, which was my old gym uniform from high school. Then I went to the kitchen to grab something to drink when I ran into Tanya.

She looked me over smiling and said, "Oh no, Miss Thang, you've got to change. We're having company, and it's a surprise."

"Not tonight. I'm tired," I replied and went to my room to lay down.

I'm not sure how much time passed as I drifted in and out of sleep, but I heard a knock at the door. Her company had arrived, but I didn't get up because I didn't feel like entertaining. So, I drifted off to sleep again. Next thing I knew, someone had smacked me on the ass, jarring me awake.

The familiar voice said, "Get up, girl!"

I opened my eyes to see Manny, Dawg, and Psycho standing in my room. I was embarrassed by them seeing me in my makeshift nightclothes.

"What are y'all doing here?" I asked.

Dawg and Psycho chuckled and smiled as if they came with gifts.

I sat up and said to Manny, "Why didn't you tell me you were coming?"

He said, "I wanted to, but your cousin told me to surprise you instead."

Manny sat down next to me while Psycho took a seat on the floor, and Dawg posted up against the wall next to the doorway. They were making small talk and joking around when Tanya came to the door.

She said, "Come here, Manny, let me talk to you for a minute."

Without question, Manny got up and followed Tanya out of the room. Now, what could she possibly want with him, I thought? I tried to listen and see if I could hear them talking, but instead, I heard the door to her room shut.

The wheels in my head started turning, and Psycho picked up on it as I glanced his way. He had a sly grin on his face that made me uncomfortable. Dawg came over and sat on the bed where Manny had been.

He said, "You smell good."

I nervously laughed off his statement and tried to change the subject.

I said, "I wonder what they're doing in there?"

I followed Dawg's glance over to Psycho. Psycho was still staring at me, but his grin had turned sinister. At that point, I was on the verge of freaking out. I got up to check and see what was taking Manny so long. When I went to walk past Psycho, he grabbed and pulled at my ankle, making me fall to the floor. Dawg laughed like that shit was funny.

Irritated, I rolled over to get up and said, "Stop, you play too much!"

Things quickly took a turn, as Psycho lunged on top of me and said, "Who said I was playing?"

Fear set in as I tried to maneuver and get him off me. I had no idea what was about to happen, nor was I trying to find out.

"Shut the door, Dawg," Psycho barked.

I was about to scream when Psycho punched me right in the face. I don't know if I was hit in the nose or the mouth, but both instantly throbbed. He hit me so hard my head snapped back and hit the floor. I saw a bright flash as if someone had taken my picture. My nose burned, and I could taste blood in my mouth. I was in trouble, and I knew it. I could no longer hold the tears back.

It felt like I was drunk, and the room was spinning.

"Please don't," I cried.

But I knew he couldn't hear me because I could barely hear myself. My lip felt really tight, and I didn't know what was wrong with me. My vision was blurry, but I could see that Psycho was about to hit my ass again. I felt a heavy-weight on my head, and I couldn't move it. I kicked my leg, and it hit the dresser knocking the items off it.

I tried to scream, but I couldn't be as loud as I wanted to. Finally, I realized Dawg had somehow maneuvered himself to the floor with us and had me in a headlock. I know Tanya had to hear the commotion, especially when shit fell off the dresser. I felt my shorts and underwear being pulled off, so I kicked my legs as hard as I could, trying to wiggle out of the vicious grip they had me in.

Psycho punched me in the stomach, and I thought I was going to die. I couldn't breathe. I couldn't scream or make a sound. I tried my hardest to scream, but nothing came out. Without warning, Psycho rammed his dick inside of me. My vagina was dry, and it felt like he was shoving sandpaper inside of me. There was no moisture, no pleasure, and only pain. I tried to claw at Dawg's arms because he was cutting off my oxygen. Somehow, he had his arm around my neck and his legs wrapped around my chest as if he were trying to put me to sleep.

Suddenly, I felt my asshole burning. Everything down there was now on fire. I stopped trying to figure out what was being done to me and started wondering how much longer I had to endure this wretchedness. I wondered how long it would be for Tanya and Manny to come to my rescue or if they were even coming.

I glanced up at Dawg and saw the tears in his eyes. It was as if they were his silent apology. Then an awful pain ripped through my gut as everything faded to black.

TO BE CONTINUED....